SQUAWWWK!

by Thomas Rockwell

Illustrated by Gail Rockwell

A YEARLING BOOK

To my mother,
Mary Barstow Rockwell

SQUAWWWK!

❦ 1 ❧

I FINISHED reading, and Miss Kinnell said, "Very good, Billy. Martha?" and Martha started,

"Suddenly the sky became dark and the sun was hidden. I imagined a cloud had passed over it, and I raised my head and saw a bird of e-e-e-*mor*mous . . ."

"E-*nor*mous, Martha."

". . . e-*nor*-mous size, bulky body, and wide wings, flying in the air, and this is what . . ."

"This it was that."

". . . this it was that concealed the sun and darkened the island. My wonder increased, and I remembered a story which travelers and voyagers had told me long before. How in certain islands there is a bird of e-e-e-*nor*-mouse . . ."

"E-nor-*muss,* Martha."

"Emormuss si —"

"E-nor-muss. Sound it out, Martha."

"E-nor-muss."

"Again."

"E-nor-muss."

"Good."

". . . a bird of e-nor-mouse size call —"

"Martha!"

"Miss Kinnell, it's a stupid word. Why don't they just say 'big'? I don't see why the people who write these dumb books always have to use such big words . . ."

"E-mor-mouse words," whispered Joe Fornaro to her behind his book.

"Nyah!" She stuck her tongue out at him.

"Children!" cried Miss Kinnell and waited for quiet. "Now. Why do you think the author used 'enormous' instead of 'big'? Jane?"

I gazed out at the rain dripping off the leaves of the

maple near the window. A gray squirrel loped across the lawn through the falling leaves. It was only ten minutes to eleven. I watched the clock. It seemed like it had been ten minutes of for an awful long time. Maybe the clock had stopped; maybe the rest of the school was already down in the gym eating lunch . . . The thick minute hand jumped. *Nine* minutes to eleven. Martha was reading again:

"A bird of e-nor-muss size called the Roc, and it feedeth its young ones with elephants."

I glanced down at my book to find the place in case Miss Kinnell called on me again (she'd make you read twice if she thought you weren't paying attention), and right over the word "Roc" there was a small black lump of something stuck to the page. It looked like a spitball at first, so I glanced over at Albert, but he was reading an Estes Rocket Catalog shoved into the opening of his desk. So I poked the thing. It was smooth and hard, like plastic. I tried to pick it off the page with my fingernail, but it was stuck to the paper. Then I tried to turn the page. But all the pages were stuck together in a lump to the back cover of the book.

So I opened my knife and laid the book flat and tried to slice the top two pages apart. No go. Then I noticed the thing was *growing,* slowly swelling up out of the

5

paper like some weird protoplasm or something, bigger and bigger, already the size of a sparrow's beak . . . I could *see* it growing!

"Billy!"

I looked up. Miss Kinnell stood over me.

"Billy, I have had to speak to you three times."

I stuck my head into the book and tried to figure out where Martha had likely left off.

"I passed the night. . . ." Miss Kinnell said.

"I passed the night sleepless," I read, and then I couldn't read any further because the thing had grown over the words.

"Miss Kinnell," I said, "can I . . ."

"Read, Billy."

"Miss Kinnell, can I go to the bathroom? I was sick last night, and now I think it's starting again."

She looked at me. I really did feel sort of sick, dizzy, my head aching.

"All right, Billy."

I slammed my book shut and went out of the room. Maybe when I came back, there'd be only a tiny stew of blood and isinglass wings on the page like a swatted fly.

I hung around the bathroom for a while, peeking through the crack at the bottom of the window at the little kids out on the playground, splashing cold water on my face, touching my toes. I just couldn't figure out what it could be, growing out of my book like that. Maybe I'd imagined the thing.

And then it came to me: a fungus. It was a fungus! Sure. Like a toadstool. The kind that spring up out of the lawn overnight. Yeah yeah.

So I went back to class.

But as I was easing the door shut carefully, like Miss Kinnell had taught us, I glanced over at my desk. The book was hopping and hitching about like a frog! And suddenly it flipped open, and there's the thing, black and shiny and as big as a goat's hoof!

It didn't look much like a fungus.

I slid into my seat, scrounging back away from the thing as far as I could, wondering if I should tell Miss Kinnell. Albert had seen it and was making faces at me behind his book, pointing at it. I shrugged *I* didn't know, and so we both watched it. Pretty soon most of the other kids sitting near me had noticed it. Then Jenny Lorimer saw it and screamed.

"Jenny! What's the matter?"

"There's something growing out of Billy's book, Miss Kinnell."

7

"Stop it, Jenny," said Miss Kinnell, coming down the aisle toward me. And then she saw it.

"Billy, what is it?"

"I don't know, Miss Kinnell. It started while Martha was reading. It just keeps on growing."

"That's ridiculous."

She snatched at it, and it split open down the middle like a beak and bit her!

She stumbled back against Martha, knocking her and her desk and chair over in a heap.

"Geez," said Albert. "I saw a *tongue*."

"Yeah," I said. I'd caught just a glimpse of it, flickering red and snakelike inside the beak.

Jenny screamed. And then Judy Schwartz did and a couple of the other girls. Martha was crying, trying to untangle herself from her desk and chair. Miss Kinnell was shaking her hand like you do when you cut your finger.

"It's bleeding, Miss Kinnell!" shrieked Judy.

It looked like pandemonium was going to break out. Everybody was up. Some were standing on their desks to get a better look; his books between his knees, Arnie Bentley was pulling on his hat at the coat closet, glancing back over his shoulder, pale and dirty-mouthed, ready to scoot if anything scary happened.

8

Lots of kids were chewing the gum they'd stored behind their ears; Amy Feldsheim was combing her hair, craning her neck to look.

But then Miss Kinnell, wrapping her handkerchief around her finger, said,

"Back to your seats, children. This *minute!* Harry, take that gum out of your mouth. Charles Hanson, WHAT do you mean? standing on your *desk!* Amy, put that comb away or I will report you to your mother again! *Everybody!* Seats! Take out your math books! Turn to page ninety-three! Problems three through five! This *instant!*"

And in about two seconds, scuffle-clatter-bang-slam-creak, everybody was in their seats, books open, slaving away at problem three: "If a car is traveling thirty-five miles an hour up . . ."

I had my math book in my lap. I couldn't lay it on my desk with that thing there. I glanced up at Miss Kinnell. She motioned to me to bring my reader up to her desk.

I put down the math book, stood up, wiped my hands on my pants, and slid my fingers gingerly under the covers of my reader. Geez, I didn't know whether it'd jump up and clamp onto my nose or what. I started off, staggering; I wanted to hold it at arm's length but it was too heavy. Albert craned up in his seat to look as I passed by, Judy Schwartz hid her face, Joe pretended he was going to pinch me.

Don't drop it, I kept whispering to myself, don't drop it . . .

I slid-heaved it onto Miss Kinnell's desk.

She gestured me back to my seat, watching till I got there, and then nodded to me to set to work in my math book.

But every so often I'd sneak a look at her. All the other kids were doing it, too. First she leaned over and smelled the thing, taking care not to get her nose too close to it. Then she poked it gently with the eraser end of a pencil, but nothing happened, so she took her ruler out of her desk drawer and gave the thing a tap. Nothing. A little harder. Still nothing. Harder. *Still* nothing. So she whapped it.

CRUNK!

The beak flashed open and crunched off the end of the ruler. It was a good, solid, wooden ruler, too, with a tin edge. And then the beak shut up again as if nothing had happened. Digesting its bite of ruler, I suppose.

She sat back, staring at it. Then she got up and emptied the class wastebasket neatly in a corner of the coat closet and set it over the beak. She put her ear to the wastebasket, listening; she tapped the side of it with a fingernail, and then with what was left of the ruler.

"Miss Kinnell?" began Albert.

"Albert," she said, glancing up, "your work."

He bent his head to his book. She waited a moment and suddenly snatched up the wastebasket. But the beak was still there. It hadn't moved or changed any, except maybe to grow a little. So she thought a moment and then opened the desk drawer she keeps her emergency supplies in — first-aid kit, flashlight, spot remover, sewing kit — and taking out her bottle of Isodine, squeezed a drop or two on the beak. The beak sneezed. She thought a moment. The whole class was watching by now.

"Tom," she said, "get me one of your sandwiches."

Tom ran.

"Now," she said, "we will try food."

I guess she'd finally decided that the beak was a strange phenomenon of nature, not just a trick some of us were trying to pull on her.

Tom dumped out his lunch bag on her desk, the orange rolling off onto the floor, and tore the wax paper off his two sandwiches.

"Ham," he said. "And egg salad."

"We will try a bit of bread first," said Miss Kinnell, tearing off a crust. "Martha, why do you suppose I am trying bread?"

"Because you think it's a bird?"

"Very good."

She stuck the crust of bread on a pencil and held it over the beak. For a minute or two nothing happened; then the beak began to nibble at it.

"Now," said Miss Kinnell when the beak had finished the crust, "we will try some ham."

But the beak wouldn't touch ham, or egg salad, or orange. Tom stuffed his lunch back into the bag.

"Barbara Loveman," said Miss Kinnell, "please bring me *your* lunch."

Barbara waited by the desk, fat and bedraggled and sheepish, standing first on one leg, then the other, while Miss Kinnell poked in her lunch bag. The rest of us all grinned and nudged each other. Finally Miss Kinnell looked up.

"Barbara," she said, "there is nothing in this bag but candy."

Everybody laughed; from the back of the room came catcalls and whistles.

"Children!"

Silence — except for the occasional muffled squeak of a chair.

"Please see me after class, Barbara."

Miss Kinnell picked a gumdrop and a candied almond out of the bag, impaled the gumdrop on her pencil and offered it to the beak. The beak ignored it. She scotch-taped the candied almond to the pencil. The beak sniffed halfheartedly at it.

"Who has an apple?" she asked, handing Barbara her lunch bag and motioning her back to her seat.

"If it wouldn't eat orange, I bet it won't eat apple," said Albert.

Jenny and Martha set apples on Miss Kinnell's desk. She examined them.

"No," she said. "Dick, did you bring an apple today?"

He nodded, scratching his elbow through the hole in his faded shirt.

"Bring it up please. Why do you think Jenny's and Martha's apples won't do?"

"Because they ain't got worms in um."

"Very good, Dick."

She laid a sheet of paper on her desk, sliced open the apple with her penknife, and extracted a fat white worm. Dick sat back down, not looking at anybody. Dick's family is real poor. They live by the town dump. The shutters are all falling off the house, and the porch roof is caved in. I've never been inside. When we go out to pick Dick up, he's always waiting out by the road, even if it's raining.

Miss Kinnell impaled the worm on the tip of her penknife and held it over the beak. *SNAP!* The beak *jumped,* the book banging against the desk. Everybody cheered.

"Wow, Miss Kinnell, that's what it likes: worms!"

"Give it another, Miss Kinnell!"

"John, what would you conclude from our feeding experiments? Sit down, Judy."

"It likes worms?"

"And bread!" shouted Joe.

"Yes," said Miss Kinnell, "we have seen that it likes bread and worms. What else have we seen?"

"It don't like oranges," said Dick.

"Or egg salad."

"Or ham."

"Or gumdrops."

"It sneezed at Isodine," whispered Arnie.

"Then it *likes* bread and worms but *dislikes* orange, ham, egg salad, and gumdrops," said Miss Kinnell. "What conclusions would you draw from that, Billy?"

"That it could be a strange bird?" I said. "Because that's what birds eat? But how could it be a bird, Miss Kinnell, when it hasn't got any wings? It's all beak."

"Good, Billy. We can conclude from our experiments that it *may* be a bird because it appears to like the same kinds of food that birds do. But we cannot say yet that it *is* a bird because it lacks the other attributes of birds — wings, feet, eyes, a feathered body."

"Miss Kinnell?" said Joe. "Can I leave the room?"
She nodded.

"Can I, too, Miss Kinnell?" I asked because I wanted

to talk over the beak with someone where we could really talk about it, you know, not have it *taught* to us like it was the law of gravity or something.

"When Joseph returns. Now children, what is the most remarkable fact about this object? What should we pay special attention to?"

"That it's coming out of Billy's book?"

"Albert?"

"That it's growing? Getting bigger?"

"Yes. We must measure its growth so that we may learn whether or not it is continuing to grow at the same rate or slowing down and perhaps reaching the end of its growth."

The noon bell rang. We could hear doors slamming, the corridors filling up.

"Children," she said, holding up her hand to keep everyone in their seats. "Please do not discuss this with students from other classes at lunch. You may discuss it among yourselves but not with others. Albert and Billy, please stay behind for a moment. Class dismissed."

So she sent me down to the cafeteria with a note, and I brought back three lunches ("Two with double ice creams," I told the serving lady. "Miss Kinnell forgot to mention it in her note.") and then she and Albert, who was good at science, made a growth scale up the wall in one corner almost to the ceiling while I lettered signs: sparrow, crow, cat, dog, sheep, pony, horse, ostrich, elephant, giraffe.

"Do you think it'll get *that* big, Miss Kinnell?" I said, watching her stretch up, standing on a chair and some books, to scotch-tape the giraffe sign to the wall way up near the ceiling. The Junior High is in the old part of the school where the ceilings are real high, over fifteen feet.

"Perhaps," she said, straightening the sign. "Turn around now while I climb down."

Then Joe and Dick came back, and she sent all of us out to the orchard behind the playground to dig worms while she went off to the teachers' room, locking the classroom behind her.

While we dug under an old apple tree, we talked about the beak. None of us could make anything of it. Joe said he figured it was from outer space, the tip of an assault force of great birdlike creatures from Orgluk.

"Orgluk?" says Albert. "What's that?"

"An undiscovered planet," says Joe, jerking his thumb at the sky. He was squatting in the hole, sifting through the loose dirt with his fingers. "The people on it have bird bodies and heads but men's legs. By tomorrow

they'll be growing up out of all the books in all the schools all over the world. People will have to climb up on the roofs of their houses to escape them. All the way down Elm Street you'll see families sitting in trees like Christmas ornaments, and the birds hopping up and down underneath, squawking in their strange, chickeny language, 'Chuck chuck chickadaa, chickadaa.'"

"You're crazy," said Albert. "How could . . ."

"Why not?" says Joe all of a sudden, looking scared. "There's thousands of planets nobody knows anything about. Have you ever heard of something growing out of a schoolbook before? *You* don't know what it is. Nobody does. Why *couldn't* it be some strange, intergalactic, four-eyed, red-nosed, chap-lipped monster? You think we oughta go home?"

"If something was invading earth, it wouldn't come out of a *schoolbook*," said Dick.

"Why not?" says Joe, glancing around behind him. "It'd be the perfect surprise attack. Like Pearl Harbor. Who'd ever expect to be attacked out of a seventh-grade *Prose and Poetry* reader?"

But Albert said that was manure, look what scientists had done to contact other planets — telescopes, rocket probes, radio receivers as big as Alley Pond — all they'd ever picked up was static. And what about the Air Force report on UFOs? What had every one of them turned out to be? Clouds, a weather balloon, optical illusions.

So pretty soon Joe quit looking behind him and grinned sort of sheepishly and said, well, yeah, maybe it *was* just a fungus or something after all.

Joe's funny about things. He'll do stuff none of the rest of us will: climb a dead tree, let us roll him down Bentley's Hill in an old tractor tire. Then all of a sudden he'll get scared by something that wouldn't scare the rest of us in six years. Like last winter we all went to a basketball game in Bennington, and coming out at half time, he got so scared by the crowd pushing and shoving all around him that he wouldn't go back in for the second half.

After we'd filled two big tomato-soup cans with worms, we squatted down to rest till the one o'clock bell rang.

Albert said, well, anyway, he figured the beak was mine, because it'd grown out of my book, and I should ask to take it home after school so we could experiment on it with his chemistry set.

But I said you couldn't tell, the book was just mine for that year, the school really *owned* it. I didn't want him to experiment on the beak; the last time he'd experimented it was making dog food out of tulips and his father's hunting dog had thrown up all over the house, and the time before that he'd burned a hole right through my mattress.

2

WELL, when Amy Feldsheim and Albert measured the beak that afternoon just before going home, it had grown eight and six-tenths inches. So we figured it was growing about four and three-tenths inches an hour and would be seventy-three and one-tenth inches high by the time we got to school at eight o'clock the next morning. Over six feet tall! Bigger than my father!

"We better tie it up or something, Miss Kinnell," I said.

"Yeah," said Joe, "if it gets that big, it could eat *us*."

"I think we must have help from a more knowledgeable person," said Miss Kinnell. "I will ask Mr. Clark to visit our class tomorrow morning. He is very knowledgeable about birds and animals."

"I still think we should tie it up," I said. "Suppose . . ."

The dismissal bell rang.

"Children," called Miss Kinnell over the rush and

clatter. "I must ask you again not to discuss this with anyone. We must not alarm others unnecessarily."

When I got home, I didn't tell my mother. I wanted to, because she sometimes knows about things, and besides, anybody'd want to talk to *someone* if a beak was growing out of his reader, and my sister Abigail is only two, no use at all. But my father was away, and if anything unusual happens when he's away, my mother gets nervous and upset and makes me stay home.

"You'll be safer at home," she'd say.

"Safer?" I'd yell. "Safer from what? Safer from the toilet running over and flooding the locker rooms like yesterday? How can I be safer from something that isn't dangerous?"

"That's enough," she'd say. "The plumbing at the school is connected to the furnace, I'm sure it is, and furnaces explode. I'll just feel safer if you're home."

So I went up to my room after supper and got out the diary my grandmother had given me last Christmas. I'd only kept it for four days:

Dec. 26: *Snow. My father argued with my mother at breakfast because she wanted to use the car tomorrow.*

Dec. 27: *Abigail fell downstairs.*

23

Dec. 28: Cloudy. Albert's yelling for me
Dec. 29: I found

I wrote down everything that had happened and drew a picture of the beak, and then I looked through my nature encyclopedia and the big bird book in the living room to see if I could match up the beak with some kind of real bird. But all the real birds' beaks were the wrong size or shape or color. So I read the parts in the back of the book about extinct birds and bird legend — the dodo, the phoenix, the griffin; how the Egyptians worshiped the Ibis; how the Greeks believed the flight of birds foretold the future.

Then I had to go upstairs to kiss Abigail good-night, and after that, I called Joe. But his brother said he'd been sent to bed early because he'd scared his little cousins with a story about a monster coming out of a book. I hung up and looked over at my mother. She was polishing silverware all over the kitchen table, dropping spoons, sighing, knocking forks onto the floor with her elbows, spilling polish and getting down on her hands and knees to wipe it up. So I went off to bed still bursting to talk.

Some kids did tell their parents, I suppose, and others were probably overheard talking on the cellar stairs with their brothers and sisters or whispering behind the platter of boiled cabbage at the dinner table. But I guess most parents figured it was a story the kids had made up or a weird school science project, because the next day only Jenny Lorimer's mother came to school, nodding and simpering at Jenny's "little friends." As soon as Mr. Swift unlocked the outside doors, we all crowded in and ran down the hall to listen at the door of our room and try to peek under the Halloween pictures Miss Kinnell had pasted on the inside of the glass. Albert had boosted Joe up to a window outside earlier, but Joe hadn't seen anything but desks and chairs before Albert's glasses had slipped down and he'd let go of Joe to push them back and Joe had tumbled down on top of him in a heap. So we milled around in the hall, wondering what had happened during the night and telling Jenny's mother and Mr. Clark about the day before till Miss Kinnell finally came and unlocked the door. We pushed in. The room looked just like it did every morning — sunlight streaming through the windows, the chairs and desks all in neat rows, Miss Kinnell's marking book right in the center of her desk blotter. We'd bedded the beak down for the night in a cardboard box, and that was still in the corner where we'd left it. But there wasn't anything in it except the

25

tattered remains of my reader. The windows were still locked, the sliding doors of the coat closet still closed. We looked all over — behind the posters and the map of the world, in all the desks; we emptied out the wastebaskets and rummaged in the supply closet, Miss Kinnell's desk drawers, the handicraft boxes. We figured it might have reversed itself and shrunk during the night instead of grown.

"Well," said Miss Kinnell finally, standing beside her ransacked desk, "it has vanished as it came. Hang up your coats. We must get to work."

Mr. Clark looked puzzled and uneasy. He probably thought we were playing a joke on him.

"What did you say it looked like, Miss Kinnell?" he asked.

"Beaklike," she said. "Joseph Fornaro, you may leave that comic book on my desk until dismissal."

"Where *is* it?" cried Jenny's mother. "I had to dress and put on my face and come all the way down here, and there's nothing to *see?*"

"No, Mrs. Lorimer," said Miss Kinnell. "There is not."

"Well, I never. I . . ."

But just then Amy Feldsheim, who was hanging her

coat in the far end of the closet like she always does, let out this

S
C
R
E
E
E
E
E
E
E
E
E
E
A
M!!

It was enough to turn your clothes inside out. Albert grabbed my arm. Then Amy

S
C
R
E
E
E
E
E
E
E
E
E
E
E
E
A
M
E
D!

again!

We looked, and she was bent double, trying to back away from the coat closet, tugging with both hands at her hair as if something inside the closet had hold of it, something nightmarish and bloody-mouthed, six-eyed and weird.

"Scissors, Mr. Clark," snapped Miss Kinnell. "Scissors."

She handed him the teacher's scissors from her desk drawer, and he ran and sheared at Amy's thick long brown hair till she staggered back, weeping and sobbing.

Then Mr. Clark backed away, the scissors poised like a sword in his hand, and we all waited, expecting whatever it was to emerge from the coat closet. But there was only silence, Amy sobbing on a chair, the creak of a window as Arnie Bentley snuck it slowly open, figuring to take his chances with the concrete five feet below rather than whatever it was in the closet.

"Does anybody have a flashlight?" asked Mr. Clark hoarsely, not taking his eyes off the closet.

"Billy."

I took the flashlight from Miss Kinnell and gave it to Mr. Clark.

"All right," he said. "Now everybody stand back. You can't tell what effect a sudden light may have on it."

He shone the flashlight into the darkness of the coat closet. Jenny Lorimer and her mother both screamed. I could hear Arnie scramble over the radiator onto the windowsill.

But you couldn't see anything at first. Except what looked like just another fur coat in the dimness. Then the flashlight moved upwards, and we saw it was a huge bird, as big as a janitor, almost six feet tall, with an enormous squat body and stubby legs and a heavy hooked beak from which draggled Amy's hair. It was blinking slowly at us, as if it didn't understand or the sudden light had dazzled it.

"Mr. Clark," said Miss Kinnell, her voice almost trembling, "you had better call Mr. Rushmore."

"Yes," said Mr. Clark and dropped the flashlight and scissors and ran out of the room.

We all waited, none of us daring to move.

CRAAAAACK! The plaster wall

30

beside the coat closet split open, the crack flickering like a snake from floor to ceiling.

"It must be still growing," whispered Albert.

The bird's head poked out into the light. Its feathers were bright blue. Its yellow beak gawked open.

SQUAWWWK!

Arnie vanished out the window. Judy Schwartz screamed. Mrs. Lorimer hid her face in her hands. There was a short-lived stampede toward the windows.

"Everybody stand *still!*" commanded Miss Kinnell. "Now. George, what would *you* want if you had been standing in the coat closet all night?"

George sniveled.

"I wanna go home."

"Judy Schwartz, stop that cowardly trembling. Harry Walters, what do *you* think?"

SQUAWWWK!

Albert and me stood our ground. But the girls and Mrs. Lorimer crowded into a corner, screaming and clawing at each other. There was a pileup near the windows when Joe tripped over a chair and George Anderson stumbled into him. Even Miss Kinnell squeaked. But then she yanked down the hem of her tweed suit jacket and thundered out:

"Harry Walters! Pay attention! What would *you*

31

want if *you* had been standing in the noat loset all kight?"

But Harry was struggling to get out from under Dick, who'd had the wind knocked out of him by Tom Conroy's knee in the pileup on top of Joe.

"Food!" thundered Miss Kinnell. "Rickles and dot hogs and peskimo sighs and —"

SQUAWWWK!

The bird waddled ponderously out into the room.

The girls and Mrs. Lorimer swooned like rag dolls in the corner, all draped limply over each other, mouths open, skirts pushed up, arms and legs all higgledy-piggledy. The worm-heap of boys convulsed spasmodically, now and then shooting a boy out and over the radiator and diving through the window. Even Albert and me stepped back, but not much.

"I bet it's a *Roc*," whispered Albert, taking off his glasses and putting them in his pocket.

"A *Roc?* Like in Sindbad? How . . ."

Just then Barbara Loveman, who'd been standing to one side all the while sucking her thumb and itching her fat hip, shrieked:

"Why's it looking at *me*, Miss Kinnell?"

". . . boast reef and morn ceal and thocolate carts and a funa-shish-falad-tandwich-on-soast!"

"Why's it looking at ME, Miss Kinnell?"

Barbara was shaking all over, the big, baby-blue bow ribbon on her dress loosening, coming undone, tears welling up in her eyes.

"He's gonna eat her," whispered Albert, all interest.

We were crouching behind an overturned desk.

"I don't know," I said.

The Roc was bobbing and turning its head to look at Barbara. It began to waddle and hop toward her through the jumble of overturned chairs and desks, the scattered papers and books.

"Why's he coming toward ME, Miss Kinnell?"

Miss Kinnell gazed distraughtly up at the ceiling. A strand of hair dangled over her face. Her lips trembled.

"Agnes Kinnell," she said softly. "Start at the beginning. A firm mind and a healthy body will sustain you through all life's crises. A firm hand, snap quizzes, and other dampening activities will keep the lid on ninety-five percent of all children between the ages of six and twelve." Her voice rose. "The remaining five percent may be dispatched to the principal's office as inveterate troublemakers or retarded. Parents may also be cowed and intimidated! Stop it, Agnes Kinnell, stop that shivering! AGNES! Not another word! I will not stand

33

for it! Open your book this minute! Silence! Detention! Double homework! Snap quiz!"

She was marching around and around her desk, waving her arms and shouting, her hair draggling over her face.

"Geez," whispered Albert. "She's flipped her lid. Look at her."

"Yeah," I said.

SQUAWWWK!

We'd forgotten the Roc. It was nuzzling Barbara's neck with its beak and then hopping back, its head cocked, to look at her. She covered her face with her hands.

"Ohhhhhhhh," she moaned fearfully, "it's going to eat me, I must look so good to eat, blue-eyed and curly-haired and plump."

But the Roc didn't even take a taste of her, just waddled all about her, nuzzling and poking her with its beak as if it expected something from her.

And then I understood the whole thing.

"He isn't *hungry*," I whispered to Albert. "He thinks she's another *Roc*. See? Her dress is blue like his feathers; she's short and fat, her dress makes her look fatter. He's in love with her, Albert. It's probably the first lady Roc he's seen in thousands of years!"

"Yeah, you know, it could be," said Albert.

All of a sudden the Roc began to circle faster and faster around Barbara, hopping clumsily into the air and flapping its stunted wings and spitting.

"Albert! It's his mating dance! It's the mating dance of the Rocs!"

"Gawd," says Albert. "I wonder what comes next."

We crouched down, waiting. The Roc hopped higher and higher, circling Barbara.

Then, *BANG!* the classroom door slammed open and in poured Mr. Rushmore, the District Custodial Superintendent, at the head of a melee of janitors and bus drivers, all armed to the teeth with push brooms, coal shovels, and pipe wrenches.

"There he is!" yells Mr. Rushmore. "CHARGE!"

Over the jumble of chairs and desks they charged like Ataturk and his Mongol hordes. But the Roc leaped straight up in the air so the whole melee passed under it, shouting and waving their pipe wrenches, and broke in confusion against the opposite wall, where they regrouped, Mr. Rushmore shouting orders, and then charged back. But just as the melee was upon it, the Roc bounded straight up into the air again, and they swept under it, coming up with shouts and blows against the blackboard.

"Steady on, boys!" yelled Mr. Rushmore, striking about him with his push broom. "Steady on. Circle him, boys, circle him. John. John, you take a squad of the bravest bus drivers, all volunteers, picked men, John, and you rush him. You rush him, he'll jump, and when he comes down, we'll be on him, me and the rest, there's vet'rans among us."

So they did, regrouping around Miss Kinnell, who was sitting at her desk by now, correcting yesterday's math quizzes and complaining querulously of the noise. But when Mr. Rushmore charged with the main body to catch the Roc when it came down, it didn't, but circled slowly, majestically, ponderously overhead, its legs walking in the air, its stunted, dodo's wings fluttering madly. Some of the pipe wrenches they heaved at it, it caught in its beak and gobbled down, weeping; others vanished into its feathers. Clambering onto a desk, Mr. Rushmore battered at the Roc's huge yellow chicken legs with a coal shovel until its handle snapped, toppling him back onto the upturned faces of his men.

"All right," yelled Mr. Rushmore, struggling up, hitting out at helping hands. "If it won't fight, we'll leave it to its own devices. John? Where's John?"

But John had collided with a falling pipe wrench and

was now staggering rubber-legged to safety in the hall, helped along by two comrades-in-arms.

"Well, then Dick. Where's Dick?"

But Dick was sprawled half in, half out of the coat closet, the victim of a rebounding push broom.

"Sam? Where's Sam?"

But two bus drivers were just dragging Sam out the door by his boots.

"Ain't nobody left?" shouted Mr. Rushmore, looking around, and then he glanced up at the Roc, still circling against the ceiling, and what happened next I shouldn't say, but it showed one of the dangers of going around looking up at big birds.

So while some of them led Mr. Rushmore off to be cleansed, others cleared the classroom, running crouching back and forth, a workbook or newspaper held open over their heads, leading out first Mrs. Lorimer and then the girls and finally searching the wreckage for survivors. And all the time the Roc circled ponderously overhead, silent and weeping.

3

OUT IN THE HALL it looked like a disaster: janitors and bus drivers and kids lying everywhichway, moaning; the school nurses moving silently among them with quart bottles of Isodine and cartons of Band-Aids; the doors of nearby classrooms stuffed with gawking, squirming children, teachers peering out over their heads. Beside the fire hose Mr. Stanwick, the Superintendent of Schools, was conferring with Mr. Firuski, the elementary principal, and the District Superintendents of Curriculum, Athletics (his name was Jack Cannon, and he'd taken off his sweat shirt and was flexing his muscles in his UCLA T-shirt and now and then jogging in place a bit as he listened), Special Programs, and Accounts.

"We got to *snuff* him out, *snuff* him out," the Cannon was saying. "Rush in there and *snuff* him out."

"How? How?" asked Mr. Spickle, the District Superintendent of Curriculum. "One must have a plan. There

38

must be a building, a progression toward a defined goal or series of goals. Start from step one, complete it, all facets and ramifications of it; then go on to step two, complete *it;* step three. And so on."

"We got to *snuff* him out, *snuff* him out," said the Cannon, bobbing and weaving, shadowboxing.

Mr. Stanwick rubbed the bridge of his nose.

"Unprecedented, unprecedented. Unforeseen, completely unforeseen."

Mr. Firuski murmured sympathetically.

"I don't know," continued Mr. Stanwick, "that I've ever seen such a situation so much as alluded to in the copious literature on school emergencies. A bird, you say?" He turned toward Mr. Clark, who was standing at a respectful distance, waiting to be called on. "A huge bird? Grew out of a boy's reader?"

Mr. Clark stepped forward a pace and then back.

"Yes, sir."

"The kid's probably a troublemaker, Chief," said Mr. Gamrow, District Superintendent of Special Programs. "If I had his name, I could put my girl on it. She'd have his file in a minute. *We'd* get to the bottom of it."

"A huge bird," mused Mr. Stanwick, still rubbing the bridge of his nose thoughtfully. "As big as a horse, you say. Not a horse painted to look like a bird, I suppose, Mr. Clark? There are precedents for horses in seventh-grade rooms."

Mr. Clark stepped forward a pace and then back.

"No, sir."

"Ah," continued Mr. Stanwick, pinching his nostrils. "Not a horse. A huge bird. Who is the teacher, Mr. Firuski? A veteran of our little yearly wars or a novice?"

Mr. Firuski closed his eyes.

"Agnes Kinnell," he recited. "Age forty-six. Born Oshkosh, Wisconsin, of white Protestant parents. Father: James Charles Kinnell, grain store clerk. Mother: Helen Carter Pollack, housewife. Education: B.A. Oshkosh

State Teachers College 1942. Experience: Fifth Grade, Provo Elementary School, September 1942–June 1944. Seventh Grade, South Sudbury Central School, September 1944–present. Academic years 1946–53: organized and conducted without compensation an after-school Special Reading Group. Academic years 1954–55: assisted without compensation in after-school Title III "Undertakings for Underachievers" program, resigning academic year 1956 when request for compensation was denied. Unmarried, childless. Emotional quotient: X_5 (stable). No pets. Staff relationships: severe but correct. Address: Manchester Gardens Apartments."

"A bird," mused Mr. Stanwick, pulling at his lips. "A huge bird."

"We got to *snuff* him out, *snuff* him out," said the Cannon, jogging in place.

"Order. Accountability. Documentation. A comprehensive system. No loose ends," said Mr. Forsythe, the District Superintendent of Accounts, with weary eyes, cleaning his glasses with his handkerchief. "If I may, sir," he said, fitting his glasses over his ears and settling them on his nose, after which he looked no longer weary but efficient, "may I suggest extermination? Perhaps a gas or insecticide of some sort? Neat. Clean. Efficient. Morally acceptable."

"Unprecedented," murmured Mr. Stanwick, pulling at the loose skin of his throat. "Unprecedented. Where is Miss Kinnell at present?"

A janitor who was standing nearby stepped up and saluted.

"With your permission, sir, she declined to leave. Said she had papers to correct, sir."

"And the bird?" asked Mr. Stanwick, humping and shrugging in his suit. "The huge bird? I suppose it is still at large in 7A?"

The janitor stepped forward again.

"Still flying about, sir."

"Gentlemen," said Mr. Stanwick, starting off briskly down the hall, the crowds of teachers and students parting before him like grass. "A public meeting must be called. This is an unprecedented situation. Should I act, it would be in an unauthorized manner. The voters must be consulted. Jack." He stopped, waiting for the Cannon to jog up, still shadow-boxing. "Jack, you're authorized to use all measures and requisition all personnel to get Miss Kinnell out of that room. Use force if you have to." He started off again, slipping on a pair of dark glasses and thrusting a corn-cob pipe into his mouth.

"He looks like General MacArthur returning to the Philippines," whispered Albert.

We were running behind him, trying to find out what was going to happen.

"Firuski. After Miss Kinnell has been removed from 7A, clear the school. Forsythe. Spickle. Gamrow. Hold yourselves in readiness. You're on the team."

Without breaking stride he plunged into the Super-intendent's suite and, trailed by three secretaries and two administrative assistants, vanished into his office.

4

W HAT'LL THEY DO?"

"I don't know," said Albert. "Come on. Let's go back and watch the Cannon rescue Miss Kinnell."

But Miss Kinnell had come out of 7A all by herself when the 9:50 bell rang, and disappeared into the teachers' room, trailed by the District Superintendent of Personnel and two crack guidance counselors. The Cannon had gone off to the gym to work out in case Mr. Stanwick ordered him to bare-hand wrestle the Roc into submission. Dick told Albert and me about it while we were jostling in the crowd out the front door toward the buses, which were idling like a herd of elephants in the driveway. Teachers and bus drivers were shouting orders; kids were yelling.

"What's going on?"

"What happened?"

"Move along there."

"Why are they letting us out early?"

"Joey Turner said a girl got her head caught in a mimeograph machine."

"Is she dead?"

"There was a fire in the seventh-grade room."

"It was a bird."

"A *bird?*"

"What kind of a . . ."

"All right, let's go, kids. Everybody on. Let's go."

Joe pushed his way through the crowd toward us.

"Come on. We'll circle around through the woods. Maybe the thing will try and break out."

I grabbed Albert, who was arguing with some eighth graders about how could a bird be *six feet tall,* for cripes sake! and the four of us slithered between the idling buses and cut down the cross-lots path through the woods so the bus drivers and teachers would think we were headed home. Just as we veered off the path, Harry Walters caught up with us.

"We're circling around," I said.

He nodded, panting.

Usually just Dick and Joe and Albert and me fool around together. Harry's a loner. But I guess anybody'd want company with something like the Roc around. We dashed up through the woods and the brambles, Joe ahead, because even though he's smaller than Albert and

45

me, he's the fastest; then Albert, who can run pretty
fast because he's tallest. But usually during the first sprint
his glasses fall off or he stumbles over a root or something. Then Dick and me because neither of us cares
who gets anywhere first and besides, his sneakers are
usually worn out. One heel's always flapping behind
and he has to sort of run-shuffle so his toes won't come
out the front. Harry always lays back; he told me once

he likes to see what he's getting into before he gets there.

At the edge of the playground we all flopped down in the bushes. The L-shaped school sat brick and quiet in the late autumn sunlight, the elementary wing nearest us. Miss Kinnell's room was in the corner of the L, the first room in the junior high–high school wing.

"Nothing doing."

"If it keeps growing, it's going to *have* to bust out."

The fire siren on top of the school let go: *weeeeee-eeeeeeee-oo, weeeeeeeeeeeeee-oo, weeeeeeeeeeeeee-oo.* Between the blasts we could hear the Mack Molding whistle and, far away, the siren on top of Carpenter's feedstore in Sandgate. That's how an emergency town meeting is called. An air raid is two whistles; an emergency town meeting is three. There's never been an air raid. My father was alive during World War II when the warning system was thought up. He says everybody was scared that the Germans were going to drop parachute troops on South Sudbury. He and my mother always laugh about it, because there's nothing strategic here, just houses and a few stores and gas stations and churches and Mack Molding, which manufactures plastic combs and crackerjack prizes. Outside the town, there's only farms and fields and the mountains.

"Look!"

Something was busting out the glass in Miss Kinnell's room. A huge yellow beak thrust out and clamped onto the window frame. The frame lurched and heaved and then shattered, tumbling out onto the grass. And suddenly the Roc's great feathered head appeared, electric-blue, its neon-yellow eyes blinking slowly, dully.

A state police car, dome light flashing, inched around the corner of the elementary wing onto the playground. Two troopers in riot helmets climbed out and crouched down behind it. Other troopers appeared on the roof.

"They've got tommy guns!" whispered Harry.

A group of men in civilian clothes came in sight around the junior-high wing. We recognized Mr. Stanwick; Mr. Firuski; Mr. Sedgwick, the high-school chemistry teacher; Mr. Clark; Mr. Langley, the chairman of the town council. They peered around the corner of the school at the Roc and then retreated and conferred. A trooper strapped on a bulletproof vest. Mr. Sedgwick and Mr. Clark handed him a window pole with something tied to the end. The trooper snuck down the wall of the school and waved the pole in front of the Roc. The Roc stared into the sky, blinking slowly, ignoring him. The trooper retreated. Mr. Clark tied a handful of hay to the pole, the trooper crept back toward the Roc.

"They're seeing what it eats."

But the Roc ignored everything they offered: an orange, a head of lettuce, candy, a string of hot dogs, a boot, Mr. Sedgwick's jacket, a mirror, a Raggedy Ann doll.

Suddenly the trooper dashed out into the middle of the playground and shouted at the Roc through a bullhorn. No response. The trooper ran up and down, waving his arms, yelling.

"That's going to be a hard bird to train," said Albert.

"They should try a big, squirming snake," said Joe.

The fire siren on top of the school gave two short blasts. Mr. Stanwick and Mr. Langley and the rest of the men in civilian clothes went off around the school. The troopers slouched against the corners of the building, their tommy guns cradled in their arms, standing guard over the Roc.

"The meeting must be starting at the town hall," said Albert.

We tramped back through the woods to School Street and then along the railroad tracks to the alley which runs down past Anderson's Five and Dime. Cars were parked along both sides of Main Street as far as you could see, and a huge crowd was pushing into the town hall through all the doors.

"We better try to hide somewhere," said Harry. "They're liable to decide kids shouldn't be allowed in."

We wormed through the crowd. Volunteer firemen were dragging folding chairs out from under the stage and setting them up in long rows. We hung back until they'd finished. Straightening up, they dusted their hands on the seats of their trousers.

"Now," whispered Harry.

We scrambled under the stage into the dusty dimness. The firemen began to bolt the gratings back over the openings.

"Hey," whispered Joe. "Are we gonna be trapped in here?"

"There's a trapdoor to the boiler room in the back," said Albert. "We can get out that way if we have to."

We crouched behind a grating, gazing out at the people walking past. Joe and Dick tried to guess who the people were by their shoes. With some it was easy. Like Mrs. Milano, who's so fat that her legs look like huge knockwursts, waddling along in dirty mashed bedroom slippers. Old Mrs. Williams's tennis shoes; Mr. Howard's old-fashioned high black dress shoes. But some none of us could tell. Most of the farmers had on overalls and big boots spattered with dried manure. There were a lot of high heels and business shoes. People tramped about overhead on the stage; the loudspeakers boomed,

"Testing, testing. One, two, three."

Harry crawled off into the darkness to explore. Joe and Dick began to argue about a pair of brown shoes which had stopped just outside the grating to talk to a pair of polka-dot shoes.

"Geez, I guess I know my own mother."

"It ain't her," said Dick. "It's Mrs. Cuspid, the school nurse."

"In brown shoes?"

"She always changes before a meeting."

"It's my *mother!*" croaked Joe. "Don't I know my own *mother?*"

"Come on," said Albert. "Cut it out. Who cares?"

Above on the stage a gavel sounded. The shoes hurried past the grating now. Chairs squeaked. The talking and chattering subsided. The meeting began.

The Reverend Eiffel and Monsignor O'Brien gave the invocation, the Girl Scout chorus sang "The Star Spangled Banner," and Mr. Langley, the chairman of the town council, announced that the meeting had been called at the request of Mr. Stanwick because of an unusually large bird at the junior high.

"I have myself visited Room 7A and viewed the bird," continued Mr. Langley. "It is certainly most unusual: approximately eight feet tall, stout, unsmiling, with bright blue feathers and long, chicken-like legs. There may, I think, be profit in it. Perhaps some zoo or circus . . ."

His voice trailed off. We could hear him pouring a glass of water, then the empty glass set down on the lectern.

"However," he resumed, "there may also be danger.

The bird is still growing. It does not appear to conduct itself like an ordinary bird. For instance, it has been observed weeping and eating chairs and has ignored Mr. Stanwick's order to leave the school grounds."

Mr. Langley paused.

"This is certainly a matter for grave consideration" — he drank some more water — "for a fruitful interchange of ideas."

He called on Mr. Stanwick for a summary of events since the discovery of the bird.

Mr. Stanwick reviewed the situation up to precisely thirteen hundred hours, when he had left his command post in the high-school science lab to come to the meeting. He then requested permission to present several members of his staff who could provide more detailed reports of various phases of the campaign. Permission was granted by acclamation. Mr. Rushmore (in clean dry clothes, I guess) perspiringly described the encounter of his raw troops with the crafty veteran bird. The Cannon described the situation from the point of view of the "athletical" department (but we couldn't hear what he said, because he was jogging right over our heads all the time: *bang bang, bang bang bang*). Mrs. Quimper, the school dietician, viewed the situation from "behind the coffee urn." Miss Kinnell viewed the situation nervously, wringing her handkerchief. Mr. Firuski . . .

But I didn't hear what Mr. Firuski had to say because Joe suddenly pitched into Dick — they'd been arguing in whispers all along, first about what color shoes Joe's mother wore, then about whether or not it was any of Dick's business, then about who had a squarer head, then about who'd like a punch in the nose, then about who was shoving who, and so on. So Harry and me had to separate them and quiet them down and finally get them to shake.

"Shhh," said Albert. "They've opened the meeting to discussion. We better listen."

"Who's talking?"

"Mr. Hill."

"Well, I guess most of you know I operate a garage over on Route 9: Hill's Auto Service Center. Now I'm not going to take up a lot of time, but when one of you brings your car in to me, say it's sputtering, or you figure there's a oil leak, there's oil on the driveway every morning. Anything. It don't matter. What do I do? *Do I call a public meeting?* Do I get on the radio and summon every man, woman, and child in town to an urgent meeting to consider Mrs. Thompson's leaking manifold? Do I call down to Mack Molding, to Mr. Speirs, and have him sound the noon siren and shut down the power so everyone can come over to the garage and study on Jack Ogden's transmission? Is that what I do?

"No, I don't. I call over Stan Griffin there, my transmission specialist, and George Syzmanski, my body man, and Bill Vale, brake and exhaust systems, and Milt Tibble there, special effects, and we stick our heads together and run a few tests and decide what needs to be done and *do it*."

He paused.

"Now ain't that the case here? Haven't we got in the budget so much for a superintendent of schools? So much for principals? So much for teachers? So much for guidance counselors, janitors, cooks, bus drivers, secretaries? Ain't it all in there? Then *I* say, let them all stick their heads together and maybe run a few tests and then decide what to do and *do it*. And let the rest of us get back to our work, for which we maybe ain't paid near as much. That's what *I* say."

"Thank you, Mr. Hill. Mr. Lusk?"

Albert groaned.

"They'll *never* decide anything if they let all the cranks talk. We'll be here till January."

Mr. Lusk's thin dry voice droned through the mumble of the crowd.

"Now there were several very interesting points in Mr. Hill's remarks but I will only focus on one just now, that one being, I have my notes here, guidance counselors, a staff appointment which has puzzled me for some time, I may have spoken of it before, the minutes no doubt will show that I have, still I would appreciate your indulgence for just a few minutes while I examine the concept once again. Guidance counselors: guide . . . counsel . . . conjunction with parents and teacher . . . I'm just running through the job description . . . knowledge of college requirements . . . admission procedures . . . here we are: degree and professional experience in psychology. The present inmates of these I believe two positions no doubt meet these requirements, Mr. Chairman, Mr. Stanwick, whoever will favor me with a reply?"

"They do, Mr. Lusk, you may be assured."

"Thank you, thank you, I'll only be a moment more, like to clarify a point or two. . . . It appears, Mr. Stanwick, that the bird is confused, eating chairs, jack-in-the-box, no appearance of molting or overindulgence in perhaps noxious foods, merely confused, requiring something, what could it be, *guidance,* Mr. Stanwick?

Guidance? Counseling, Mr. Stanwick? Counseling? Those students who are unable to adjust to the patterns, I am reading again from the job description, of behavior established by the community, board of education and faculty, and here perhaps we come to the nub of what I am trying to suggest, *shall be counseled by the,* I beg your attention, *guidance counselors.* I submit that this is the case with our friend the bird. *Has anyone tried to reason with him?* Thank you."

"May I reply?"

"Mr. George Snatchly, our senior guidance counselor. Mr. Snatchly."

"From its first beginnings in a casual word of advice from teacher to pupil in a log cabin somewhere in the wilderness of what would later become the great state of Illinois . . ."

Harry fell asleep on his back. Joe and Dick played tic-tac-toe in the dust, and odds and evens, and Indian-wrestled. Albert listened at the grating.

For a while I listened with him, but most of the time people were just arguing about whose turn it was to speak or making dumb suggestions: an old lady way in the back asked that the Roc be paroled in the custody of the local chapter of the Audubon Society, of which she was president and treasurer; Mr. Weyerhauser said he'd been a chicken farmer all his life, forty-five years man and boy, never yet see a bird he couldn't handle, he'd take it on; if it laid eggs, they'd all be rich, think of the size of the eggs; a lot of people had ideas about how to spend the money that the town was going to make by exhibiting the Roc; women kept asking silly questions, like will it eat my new Barcalounger? or, will the Library Society meet tonight as scheduled? or, her first cousins were coming over from Proctor for a visit that evening, should she ask them to wait till next week? Finally a man got up and said he couldn't stand to sit there anymore and listen to all this frivolous talk and chatter, he wanted action, otherwise he was going home. So another man asked him nastily, if he was so smart, what action did he suggest? So the first man said he'd never claimed to be smarter than anyone else, but he knew one thing: the situation cried out for a remedy; as far as he could see . . . The other man asked how far that was? So Mr. Secor said Harvey Cooper hadn't no right to interrupt like that, everybody should be allowed to speak his piece.

Every so often a state trooper would come in to report that the Roc was still growing. Now it was fifteen feet tall, now eighteen, now twenty. Then there'd be a flurry of concern, calls for action, shouts of "Vote, vote!" But pretty soon the meeting would bog down again. All across the crowd you could see people eating lunch or reading newspapers or sleeping peacefully, slumped against a wife's or neighbor's shoulder.

I lay back in the lint and dust, wondering what would happen. Suppose the Roc turned out to be a kind of owl that hunted people like mice and rabbits so we all had to live underground and only come out of our holes on rainy nights when there was no moon? Or suppose it never stopped growing? The government would build bigger and bigger cages for it, at the last using dirigibles to lower the mammoth girders into place. Pretty soon the Roc would be so incredibly huge —bigger than New York City piled on top of Los

Angeles piled on top of Shanghai piled on top of St. Louis, with all their noisy crowds and skyscrapers and tenements and garbage dumps and subways and bridges and traffic jams and factories — that the earth would start to sink slowly through space because of the extra weight — past Mars, Jupiter . . . picking up speed, faster and faster . . . Saturn, Uranus, Neptune . . . My father'd stay home all the time at first. We'd sit up all night listening to the radio and looking through telescopes, watching the strange galaxies slide by. Then gradually things would go back to normal. Schools and factories would reopen; my mother's bridge club would begin to meet on Thursday afternoons again. Suddenly the Roc would fly off, marooning earth in a strange galaxy where all the other planets were square. There'd be . . .

Or suppose the earth began to cave in under the Roc. He'd be squawking, his head in the clouds, while under him, in the shadows where no sunlight penetrated, mountains, fields, and cities slid into the widening pucker around his feet: Rutland, the railway yards at White River Junction, Mount Greylock, the Schoharie County Fair — its deserted midway and refreshment stands, long tables piled high with wormy prize pumpkins and rotting pies, a last looter fleeing across a field before the sliding, crumbling earth.

And then, suddenly, the earth's crust would split open, and the Roc would plunge out of sight into the fiery core, Lake George, Sacandaga Reservoir, and the Hudson River pouring in behind him, gushing and foaming through the last sliding, toppling remnants of Albany. A vast cloud of steam would arise, blanketing the eastern United States. Airports would be closed; looters would roam the streets of major cities, fighting pitched battles with the police and National Guard in the murky vastnesses of Macy's and Sears, Roebuck. And night and day, from the Great Pucker would rise a low, steady bubble-glubble, bubble-glubble like distant thunder.

And then, six days later, as the first planes were landing in Cincinnati and the Twenty-second Airborne was mopping up the last pockets of resistance in the dry-goods department of Bamberger's — faraway, in a small town on the west coast of Ireland, it would begin to rain chicken soup . . .

Joe was shaking me by the shoulder.

"Come on. We're going to have a spitting contest. Hey. You sleeping with your eyes open?"

So Joe and Dick and me had a spitting contest, and it was tied three all in the noisy fourth when Albert said,

"Shhh. Rushmore just ran in."

"The bird, ladies and gentlemen," cried Mr. Langley overhead. "We *must* decide on a definite course of action. Mr. Rushmore has just come from the school and reports that the bird is now more than thirty-five feet tall and still growing. Room 7A is a shambles. Mr. Stanwick, may we hear now from our student council representatives?"

❧ 5 ❧

MISS CARGILL, president of the student council."

I ducked down so I could look through the grating. Doris Cargill was standing up in the front row with her books in her arms, waiting for quiet, staring straight ahead through her thick glasses. None of us younger kids liked her. She was always hissing at us to *"shut up"* or *"stand still."* When the hall was quiet, she licked her lips and read from an index card sticking out of one of her books:

"Mr. Stanwick, ladies and gentlemen. As president of the student council, I'd just like to say that I think the staff of South Sudbury Central School performed miracles in getting us all out safely this morning. But it's just another example of the bang-up job they do every day. I think they are the most dedicated, hardworking bunch of people any of us have ever known. Sometimes when you're visiting our school, you'll see an eighth grader yelling in the halls or some fifth graders

63

running up the stairs from the gym. But let me assure you that's no reflection on our fine staff. It's just youthful high jinks. We're overflowing with high spirits because we love our school and our teachers and all of you who have made this possible."

She glanced down at the index card.

"Thank you for letting me speak. Mr. Wilson, our fine speech teacher, always chuckles in speech class when one of us gets carried away and goes on too long. He chuckles and says, 'Better late than never.' So then we have to laugh, too, even the one who's gone on too long. So I'll stop now, before I've gone on too long. But I just want to say that we really appreciate the wonderful school you've given us and our really dedicated, top-notch teachers. Thank you."

The town hall rang with applause and huzzahs.

"Whoopee," said Albert.

"Yeah," said Dick.

"Boy, is she a *fink!*" said Harry. "A *fink!*"

"Miss O'Connor, treasurer of our student council."

"Mr. Stanwick, should I give my monthly treasurer's report or just, you know, say something general?"

"General, Miss O'Connor, general. We'd like to know what the student body feels at this juncture."

"Well, Mr. Stanwick, I agree with everything that

Doris said. I mean, we couldn't ask for better teachers. Sometimes they tell jokes right in the middle of class. I mean, it's real fun to learn in this school. It's funsville. And we know we're going to be better persons when we leave. I mean, patriotic and dedicated and, I mean, real *thoughtful* young men and women. Is that all right? I mean, is that the sort of thing you wanted? I usually don't have to make the speeches. Doris does. Or Harold."

"Thank you, Miss O'Connor. Mr. Furst, may we have your thoughts. Mr. Harold Furst, vice-president of our student council."

"I'd just like to remind everybody that this Saturday the South Sudbury Saberjets will journey to Woronsick to take on the Woronsick Tigers. Speculation has it that the Tigers are fired up for this one and really want revenge for last year's seven-to-thirty shellacking. But Coach Cannon" — youthful cheers broke out like measles all across the hall — "and our eleven have a few tricks up their sleeves too. So let's give them a real hip-hip-hurrah. Ready? HIP-HIP-HURRAH! SOUTH SUDBURY! SOUTH SUDBURY! EAT EM UP, EAT EM UP, EAT EM UP! *YAAAAHHHHHH!* That was great. Now other events on tap for the weekend are: girls' volleyball against Valley Stream, River-

view Field, 2 P.M. sharp; boys' soccer against Ancram-
dale at 3 P.M.; and a cross-country meet at Salem High
at 3:15. I'd just like to add that I've polled the other
members of the football team and we're all unanimous
that if you want us to take on that bird or whatever it
is, we'll do it. Coach Cannon" — youthful cheers — "has
got a play worked out, and we'd really like to try it. It's
the only play we've ever had where both the defensive
and offensive teams get to be in the game at the same
time, so we'd really like to try it. And it won't make any
difference to Saturday's game because we can eat up
them Woronsick Tigers with both hands tied behind
our backs and blindfolded."

Youthful cheers, foot stampings.

A man jumped up in the back.

"Mr. Langley. Mr. Langley."

"Mr. Cummings?"

"Mr. Langley, I'd just like to say that that's one of the
finest statements I've ever heard. And I'd like to offer
my personal congratulations to Coach Cannon" —
youthful cheers — "and the team. Bring on them Woronsick Tigers!"

Thunderous applause.

"I am sure," intoned Mr. Langley, "now that we have
heard these comprehensive statements by the officers of

our student council, that we all feel that the future of our country is in good hands and that our way of life will be carried into the next generation without substantial alteration. Excuse me."

A state trooper ran past the grating. There was a whispered conference on the stage.

"Ladies and gentlemen, Officer Henderson has just informed me that the bird grew twenty-five feet in the last half hour! Ladies and gentlemen, I call upon you to vote now, now while there is still time! All in fav —"

"Vote?" shouted a man. "Before I've had a chance to speak my piece? That ain't —"

"Mr. Fisk, this no time for quibbling. There is not a moment to lose."

Several voices shouted,

"Vote!"

Vote!"

"What are they going to vote on?" I asked Albert.

"Nothing. They've just been talking and talking. They've forgotten that nobody's made a motion yet."

More voices shouted,

"VOTE!"

"Vote!"

"Vote!"

"VOTE!"

The crowd was panicking. Mr. Langley shouted,

"All those in favor?"

There was a thunderous chorus of "aye!"

"All those opposed?"

There was a thunderous chorus of "nay!"

Confusion. Shouts of "Roll call! Roll call!" Fistfights broke out here and there in the crowded hall.

"A show of hands, ladies and gentlemen, let's have a show of hands. All those in favor?"

A forest of hands went up. Mr. Stanwick, Mr. Firuski, Mr. Spickle, and Mr. Forsythe were delegated to do the counting. While they proceeded slowly down the aisles, a herd of cooks, cooks' helpers, and dishwashers from the school cafeteria, busily directed by Mrs. Quimper, served coffee and doughnuts from thermos carts.

"You mean they aren't voting on *anything?*" asked Harry.

"About forty people made suggestions, most of them stupid — you heard them — and then they called on those student council finks, and then the trooper ran in. It's like all grown-up meetings: they talk and talk and talk, and argue and argue and argue, and nothing gets done."

"But how can they vote on *nothing?*"

"They're panicking," I said.

"Maybe they're *right,*" said Joe suddenly, in a squeaky voice. "*People's* appetites change as they get older, don't they? The Roc didn't eat furniture at first. Remember the bread and the worms? Maybe now it wants *flesh! Human flesh!*"

We all looked at each other in the dimness.

"Oh, come on?" said Harry doubtfully.

"So what?" said Albert. "Before it finishes all the people out front, we can escape through the trapdoor to the boiler room."

"Yeah," I said. "And besides, I don't believe it'll eat people anyway. The Roc in Sindbad didn't, and when the state trooper was experimenting to see what this one would eat, it acted like it didn't know he even existed. Like he was in a different time warp or something."

We turned back to the grating. Mr. Stanwick, Mr. Firuski, Mr. Spickle, and Mr. Forsythe were reporting the count.

"All those opposed?"

While the counting resumed, people began folding up the chairs in the back rows. The lights in the hall were turned on, for it was now late afternoon, and the sky outside was dark with rushing clouds. The wind whistled across the roof of the hall; windows creaked.

"Ladies and gentlemen, the ayes have it."

A cheer went up, drowning the fierce rushing of the wind for a moment. Mr. Langley rapped for order.

"I think we may all congratulate ourselves on our afternoon's work. Once again the democratic process has been vindicated. Ladies and gentlemen, I salute you. What? Mr. Edgerton? You wish to speak? What more is there to say? Mr. Stanwick, is this . . . ? All right, all right. Speak, speak, Mr. Edgerton, so that we may all go home. Out with it, out with it."

Mr. Edgerton, our English teacher, spoke above the confused murmur of the munching, sipping crowd.

"What has been decided?"

"What has been decided? Come, come, Mr. Edgerton.

Surely you were present when the vote was taken. Surely he was present, Mr. Stanwick?"

"He was. Mr. Edgerton, we'll have no more of this. I observed you standing just behind Mr. Andrews throughout the meeting."

"I only ask one simple question: What has been decided? It is . . . that is, it is very difficult to hear from this side. Could not the substance, just the substance, of the meeting's decision be repeated for the benefit of those of us on this side?"

"Ah. Yes, yes, of course. We had assumed that you were raising a doubt, a scruple. Mr. Stanwick, would you just summarize for us. I am sure we would *all* benefit from such a summary."

"Certainly. Certainly. Just give me a moment to collect my thoughts. Yes. Certainly . . . Yes . . . Ah . . . Now . . . Well, I, I do not seem able to quite frame it in just the right words. Such a momentous decision . . . do it justice . . . Perhaps Mr. Firuski will do us the honor of summarizing *his* view of this awesome decision while I gather my thoughts? Mr. Firuski."

"Yes . . . That is . . . Yes. Yes. I ah rather think this deserves, cries out for . . . only Mr. Wilson, our golden-tongued speech teacher, could do a decision of this magnitude justice. Mr. Wilson."

"For the first time in my career I must confess, Mr. Firuski, though to do so is the most excruciatingly painful experience of that career, that I am, in short, at a loss for words. I can only throw the ball back to you, Mr. Stanwick."

"What has been decided?" asked Mr. Edgerton into the dead silence of the hall.

The wind roared and whistled on the roof. Even Mrs. Quimper had fallen silent. Coffee cups were poised on lips; hands hung motionless above plates of doughnuts.

"What has been decided?"

Through the grating, unable to contain himself a moment longer, Albert squeaked:

"Nothing!"

"Nothing," echoed Mr. Edgerton. "You fools. Nothing. At the eleventh hour: nothing. You have voted for emptiness, a void, a silence."

The wind moaned on the roof. Somewhere a shutter banged and clattered.

"Come," cried Mr. Edgerton. "There may still be time. Come. Let us gather ourselves together. Now. There may still be time."

But as his last words echoed through the silent hall, there came, from just outside:

SQUAWK!

A brick tumbled out of the wall. Another. A tiny waterfall of dust. The wall bulged.

"Run!" shouted Mr. Rushmore, plunging into the hall through a side exit. "Run! It's broken out! One hundred feet high, electric blue, its basketball eyes glowing in the dark. Run! Run!"

The crowd broke, surging toward the doors. A thermos cart toppled, flooding steaming coffee under running frantic feet.

"Women and children first, women and children first!" shouted Mr. Stanwick, thrusting his way through the crowd toward the door.

"Form a line of defense at the far wall!" yelled Mr. Langley, gesturing frantically back over his shoulder as he labored through the frenzied crowd toward an exit.

"Pray! Pray!" yelled Monsignor O'Brien and Reverend Eiffel, the latter boosting the former out a window.

Feet trampled across the stage over our heads. The

fire alarm clanged and clanged. Peering out through the grating, we could see children clinging like flies above the tumult on windowsills and coat hooks. Joe's cousin Tony perched on a loudspeaker box, calmly surveying the crowd and now and then spitting experimentally down into the bedlam of shouts, screams, wails, and strangled cries.

Albert grabbed me, yelling "Come on!" and pulling me away from the grating, and I turned and caught a glimpse of Harry and Dick crowding down a trapdoor far back in the dimness under the stage. Stooping, Albert and I ran after them and dropped through, landing in a heap beside the furnace. Scrambling up, we flung up the stairs and out into the parking lot. Snow swirled and eddied in the floodlights.

"Around to the front!" yelled Joe, flinging up his arm like General Custer and dashing off. We rushed after him.

The crowd poured from doors and windows, streaming across the snowy lawn and down the hill, whitefaced, groaning with fear. Over the roof of the town hall, through the whirling snow, the Roc stared down at them.

"By George," yelled an old man, stopping to shake his palsied fist at the Roc, "you'll pay for this!"

He dashed on.

Mr. Stanwick and Mr. Rushmore crouched behind the fenders of their Cadillacs, staring up at the Roc. Mrs. Quimper ran past carrying a tray of jelly doughnuts to safety. We could see the Cannon forming up the football team behind the maple tree at the far end of the parking lot.

Occasionally someone in the crowd paused to glance back and then, seeing the Roc's head and glowing yellow eyes swiveling slowly back and forth over the roof of the town hall, ran on with renewed vigor. Soon gaps began to appear in the crowd. Old men and women were seen struggling along. Fathers carrying two and sometimes three children staggered past. And then suddenly we were alone — the five of us — on the trampled snow of the driveway. We glanced back. There was only whirling snow in the darkness above the town hall. The Roc had disappeared. The charging football team pulled up in confusion before the front steps.

"Come on," yelled Albert. "Around to the back!"

"How do you know it's not dangerous?" shouted Joe. Albert yelled over his shoulder.

"It hasn't done anything yet! Let's see where it went."

6

Pᴌᴜɴɢɪɴɢ around the corner, I collided with Albert, who had pulled up short in the dark. He was watching a man peering around the opposite corner.

"It's a state trooper," he whispered.

Behind us a car door slammed. Another trooper came running around the corner, carrying a submachine gun. We flattened ourselves against the wall.

"Which way'd he go?" said the second trooper.

"Back up the hill."

"We better follow him. Where's Sam?"

Albert pushed me and Joe back around the corner. A deserted state police car idled in the falling snow, its doors hanging open.

"Quick. Get in and lie down. We can ride back to the school with them."

So we all piled in and scrounged up together in the shadow behind the front seat. Pretty soon the two state troopers came running back and jumped in, flinging their submachine guns onto the back seat.

At the school we waited till we couldn't hear their boots crunching in the gravel and then peeked out over the seat. The yard was jammed with state police cars. We slid out and around through the woods. Crawling under the snow-covered bushes, we peered out into the floodlit playground. Snow squalls swept out of the darkness, breaking against the school, flaring up and over it. The Roc was hopping about outside the first-grade room, eating playground equipment. *Chomp!* The teeter-totter crumpled. The Roc stood stock still for an instant, then threw back its head; a jagged lump slid down its chickeny throat.

"Look!" squeaked Joe.

Troopers dashed out onto the playground from around the corners of the school and crouched or flung themselves down in the snow, leveling tear-gas guns, rifles, submachine guns, shotguns at the Roc.

A bullhorn boomed:

"FIRE!"

Ta-ta-ta-ta-ta-ta-ta-ta-tat, *ca-pow, ca-pow,* ta-ta-ta-ta-ta-ta-ta-ta-ta-ta-ta-ta-ta-ta-ta-ta-ta-ta-ta-ta-tat-tat-tat . . . *boom-sloosh* . . . *boom-sloosh.* Tear-gas canisters arched through the falling snow. Bullets ricocheted off the

Roc's yellow beak and kicked up snow and turf around its feet. It began to dance clumsily about like a hoopoe.

Then it caught sight of the arching tear-gas canisters and stopped, watching them spinning toward it, bounding across the snow. A canister exploded by its feet; for a moment the Roc was hidden in a boiling cloud of gas. Then suddenly it danced out of the cloud and, opening its beak, caught a canister in midair and swallowed it. There was a dull boom as the canister exploded in the Roc's stomach. Wisps of gas leaked from the corners of its beak. It caught another canister, and another, bullets ricocheting off its beak, rumpling and ruffling through its feathers.

"They're crazy," said Joe. "It's like trying to kill an elephant with spitballs."

The guns fell silent. The troopers retreated haphazardly around the corners of the school. The Roc stopped dancing and began to peck at a jungle gym.

The bullhorn boomed:

"Troop Five, first watch. Troop Six, withdraw to the gymnasium."

Troopers squatted at the corners of the school, watching the Roc, their submachine guns laid across their knees. Behind them other troopers and a few janitors dragged chairs and desks out of the school and, dousing them with gasoline, kindled watch fires, and then stood around them, warming their hands, stamping.

"Let's go," said Joe. "Nothing else'll happen tonight."

"Wait. See what the Roc does."

The catastrophically huge, electric-blue bird gulped down the last bent pipes of the jungle gym and began to preen, poking and smoothing busily in its feathers with its beak. Once or twice it lifted its head and burped; nuts, bolts, and chain links shot out of its beak into the darkness. Then it gawped and began to waddle round and round in one spot, sinking to its knobby knees, settling down onto the snowy grass. Its blue, membranous eyelids closed; it ruffled its wing feathers, gawped, burrowed its beak into its wing, sighed, and was still. Gradually the snow whitened on the monstrous, electric-blue mound in the glare of the floodlights. Soon it resembled a small, snow-covered hill.

"Come on," said Albert. "We'd better head home."

We went down through the woods. A school bus was picking up stragglers from the panic at the town hall.

"Where were you?" asked my mother. She was feeding Abigail in her high chair in the kitchen. "I was beginning to worry."

"A huge bird got into the school," I said. "They held a big meeting at the town hall about it."

I figured even if she hadn't heard about the Roc, it'd be on the evening news so I'd better ease her into it.

"Eat your toast, dear," she said to Abigail. "What kind of a bird?"

"A Roc."

"You mean like in Sindbad the Sailor?"

"Yeah. Can I have some more crackers?"

"Finish your soup first. I made it specially. How could it be a Roc? Rocs don't exist."

"This one does. You should have seen it knock down the wall of Miss Kinnell's room. Bammo! And then it ate some chairs and a jungle gym. I bet there won't be any school tomorrow."

"Are you sure you're not making this up?"

"Turn on the radio. You'll see. Bammo! Down went the wall! And you should have seen everybody run when it squawked outside the town hall during the meeting. All the fat old ladies, Monsignor O'Brien and old Stanwick and Firuski, shoving and pushing."

"Young man, are you lying to me? What's this all about? Mr. Stanwick and Mr. Firuski and Monsignor O'Brien running and pushing?"

"It's true. Turn on the radio if you don't believe me."

Click.

"I certainly will. And your father in California. Oh dear."

But there was nothing on the radio about it. Just the war in Vietnam and inflation and a report of a test of a hydrogen bomb in China.

"It *did* happen! It *did!* You saw how late I came home! Didn't you see Mr. Terwilliger driving the bus? He *never* drives my bus. Call up Mrs. Loveman, Barbara's mother. She'll tell you. She lives right near the school."

"If you're lying, young man . . ."

The phone was dead.

"I bet the Roc . . ."

"That's *enough!* Trying to frighten Abigail and me when your father isn't home. Up to bed! This minute!"

There was a knock at the door. I slid around behind Abigail and edged toward the door to the woodshed. I wasn't going to get locked in my room till morning. Harry and Joe and Dick and Albert and me had agreed to meet in the woods back of school an hour before daylight. We wanted to see what happened when the Roc woke up.

"Mrs. O'Reilly. How nice to see you."

It was Albert's mother. Albert slid around her into the kitchen.

"Mrs. Travis, I'm sorry to trouble you. Albert came home with this wild story . . ."

"Oh yes. Billy, too." She glanced around at me. Albert and me were inching toward the door of the woodshed. "You may stay up, since Albert is here. But no funny business."

"I thought so, too," said Mrs. O'Reilly. "But then Tom Fortune came by, knowing my John was away, and told me it's true. There's some kind of a huge bird at the school. It's torn down some walls and eaten tables and chairs. He had it from Mr. Terwilliger, the bus driver, who saw it with his own eyes. The National Guard has been called out, and the Governor and General Westinghouse are supposed to be flying in by helicopter."

"Have they shut off the telephones?"

"Yes. They don't want word to get out. There might be a panic tomorrow on the stock exchanges. Or the Russians might try to take advantage."

"Oh dear. Is it a dangerous bird? I mean, does it eat people?"

"Mr. Terwilliger didn't think so. He said it had lots

of chances to but hadn't tried to even taste anybody, not even one of the kindergartners. He thinks it will fly away in the morning. He thinks it's from outer space somewhere and got lost."

"Oh dear. And Billy's father is in San Francisco and won't be back for three days."

"That's what I thought, Mrs. Travis. I wondered if you'd like Albert and I to stay with you tonight. Albert could keep Billy company, and we could take turns watching out for things."

"Oh, would you, Mrs. O'Reilly? I'd be so grateful. This is such a big house."

And so Albert and me slept together in the big bed that night, the alarm clock ticking under the covers between us, set for 4 A.M.

❧ 7 ❧

BUT IT WAS the cough and roar of engines that woke us. We hopped out of bed in the darkness and, peeking under the shades, saw a blacked-out convoy of tanks and missile launchers and weapons carriers, scooting jeeps, and truck after truck after truck, lumbering up the Cambridge–South Sudbury highway. A helicopter hung over the covered bridge, red lights blinking, and then suddenly dipped and slid away into the night.

"Wow," I said.

"Let's count them."

The door opened behind us.

"Bed," said my mother.

"Geez, Mom, did you see the *tanks*? And the missile launchers?"

"Bed."

We crawled back under the covers. She tucked us in.

"Do you think there'll be school tomorrow, Mom?"

"I don't know, Billy. Now go to sleep."

After she'd closed the door, we snuck a look at the clock. It was quarter of three.

"Let's go now," I said.

"We better sleep some more. We'll be too tired otherwise."

But I couldn't sleep. After a while, I whispered, "I can't sleep. Can you?"

"I could if you'd shut up."

I lay still, listening to the endless rumble of the convoy on the highway. Occasionally a helicopter would clatter by overhead.

"I'm going to get up and look at the tanks again."

I started to throw back the covers. Albert grabbed me.

"No. We got to pretend we're asleep. Otherwise they'll separate us."

I lay back.

"What do you do to try to go to sleep?"

"Sometimes I tell myself stories."

"Yeah. What are your stories about?"

"Oh, things. You know, wars and baseball and things."

"Yeah."

We were silent a bit, listening to the rumble of the convoy.

"I bet you're always the he-ro," whispered Albert, poking me in the stomach and giggling.

So we wrestled under the covers, trying to tickle each other until Albert laughed right out.

"Shhh. Cut it out. They'll separate us."

So we lay back, panting, now and then bursting into giggles again.

"I'll bet you're always *your* hero, too," I whispered.

Albert made a noise like a machine gun.

"Sergeant O'Reilly zigzagging up Limerick Street, gunning down the Black and Tans. Kush-*hing,* kush-*hing*. Bullets ricocheting around his feet. Boom! Behind him, the British command post explodes in flame."

"What war is that?"

"The Irish Revolution. It was a neat war. Guerrilla fighting, trains and bridges blowing up, a lot of every-man-for-himself stuff, cornered, out-manned, out-gunned, hostages pleading for mercy."

"Who was fighting?"

So he told me about the Irish Revolution till the alarm muffled off under my pillow. Then we got into our clothes and snuck down the back stairs, listening at every step. Our mothers were sleeping in rocking chairs beside the kitchen table. My father's shotgun lay on the table between them.

"Maybe we better leave a note."

"Yeah."

So Albert wrote a note saying we'd gone to school early because we couldn't sleep and I snuck in and slid it under the barrel of the shotgun. Then we set off. The snow had changed to a drizzle, and the road was deserted, the night still except for an occasional helicopter in the distance. At the Sandgate crossroads we waited under the lightning-blasted tree and pretty soon along came Dick. Joe was waiting outside his garage, and Harry was already crouched behind a tree, staring into the floodlit playground through his father's binoculars.

"What's happening?"

"Nothing. I been here half an hour and it hasn't moved."

"Can you see it breathe?"

We all watched the gigantic snow-covered mound beside the school.

"Lemme try the binoculars."

"Yeah, it's breathing. Sure. See? On the side toward the gym?"

"Lemme have a look."

"Where'd they set up the missile launchers and stuff?"

"They're camped on the baseball field. Down the hill in front."

"Let's go see. Come on."

"Somebody's got to watch the Roc."

But nobody wanted to miss seeing the tanks and missile launchers close up, so we decided the National Guard would be watching the Roc, and we'd know soon enough if it started something.

Down the hill in front of the school there were trucks and jeeps parked all along both sides of School Street. Squads of tanks, their engines idling, blocked the two entrances to the school driveway. Soldiers were digging machine-gun pits in the clusters of barberry bushes near the tanks, and a whole platoon was deployed around the flagpole on the lawn in front of the school to cover some men digging a forward observation trench. The baseball field was crawling with vehicles; men were digging trenches and latrines, setting up tents and unloading supplies, walking about, shouting orders. Here and there a truck was mired to the fenders, surrounded by a crowd of soldiers leaning on shovels and picks. The truck's engine would be roaring, its wheels spinning, spitting mud.

We skirted through the woods around the tanks in the driveway and dashed across the road. Dawn was breaking in the east behind us, gray and muddy. We stopped to look at a tank, walking slowly all around it, daring each other to climb on.

"Hey, you kids."

A Green Beret came through the drizzle toward us.

"You kids should be home in bed."

The Green Beret lifted Dick, who was the littlest, onto the fender of the tank.

"You're liable to get run over," he said. "All these tanks and trucks. Aren't you up sort of early?"

Grown-ups always think kids are going to get run over. I bet more of them than us are run over every year, walking around fat and old and half blind and crippled and drunk, wobbling along on high heels . . .

"Where do you boys live?"

We shrugged, sort of gesturing off behind us.

"You want to stay and see the fun, eh?"

He looked down at us. Boy, was he *big!* And his shirt all covered with medals and ribbons.

"Follow me."

He started away through the tanks. We trailed behind. If it'd been a teacher or someone, we'd have cut and run, but you know, he was a Green Beret — trousers

tucked into his paratrooper boots, lanyard, dagger, pistol, face blackened and hideous.

"I guess you were pretty scared yesterday when that bird chased you out of the school?"

"Naw," said Joe. "We wasn't scared."

"Naw."

"Naw."

"Naw."

"Naw."

"We watched the state troops find out what it likes to eat."

"Yeah, they fed it boots and rosebushes and a riot helmet. We think it's a Roc."

We were slogging through the mud behind the Green Beret, swaggering a bit. Boy, was he *big!* His neck was like, I don't know, you could see the muscles ripple in it whenever he turned his head.

"Like in Sindbad the Sailor."

"Sindbad ties himself to its leg and the Roc carries him miles and miles to the Valley of the Diamonds."

We rounded the back of a truck. Harry groaned. I bit my lip. Mr. Stanwick and Mr. Firuski waited in galoshes and raincoats, with plastic covers on their hats, behind a group of officers bent over a map table. You could see they weren't comfortable in the rain and mud like the Green Beret and us.

"What's this?" said Mr. Stanwick, catching sight of us. "Mr. Firuski. What's this?"

"Impudence," said Mr. Firuski. "Albert O'Reilly, don't move. Impudence and bad manners. Inveterate hatred of authority. Reckless disregard for the feelings of others. An incorrigible willingness to step beyond the bounds of common decency. Bad-mindedness. Self-indulgence. Obstinacy."

He grabbed Harry by the shoulder.

"Here's Henry Walters," he said.

"Ah," said Mr. Stanwick, "so that's Henry Walters, is it?"

"None other," said Mr. Firuski.

"Ah," said Mr. Stanwick, "I would have suspected it even if you hadn't told me. He has a look about him."

"And this," said Mr. Firuski, pushing Joe forward, "is Joseph Fornaro."

"Who else?" said Mr. Stanwick, pulling his nose. "Who else? With that inveterate darkness around the eyes." He pointed at Dick. "And that one? With the dirty hair? Don't tell me, I'll guess.

Pale, bony face. Worn leather jacket two sizes too small, ragged cuffs. Chapped hands. The drunkard's son, Richard —"

Dick flung himself at Mr. Stanwick. But Mr. Stanwick clapped his hand down on Dick's head and held him off. Dick butted against the hand, flailing away, trying to reach the raincoated stomach.

"Here," said the Green Beret, picking up Dick and setting him away from Mr. Stanwick. "Hold on, boy. You're not making much headway."

"Moore," said Mr. Stanwick. "Richard Moore, the drunkard's son. The boy with the *mysterious* sisters."

Dick SCREAMED! And it's a good thing the Green Beret had hold of him because he would have flung himself at Mr. Stanwick again. We all would have if we'd thought we had a chance. Albert said afterwards he would have. And Joe had hated Mr. Stanwick ever since he'd kicked Joe's older brother out of school for smoking in the locker room.

"You're the principal?" said the Green Beret, holding Dick back.

"The superintendent, officer," said Mr. Stanwick. "My colleague here, Mr. Firuski, is the elementary principal."

"Well," he said, "you'll have to excuse us then, because I got to take my cousin here and his friends home.

95

They shouldn't ought to be wandering around here, with that bird loose. You boys come on with me now."

And he started off and us after him. Except he was pulling Dick along by the arm because Dick was still struggling to get away and fling himself at Mr. Stanwick.

The Green Beret led us off to the edge of the field toward town and pointed down the street.

"Now," he says, "you get on home, you hear? I got you off that time because I was in school once myself. Straight home now."

So we said sure and thanked him. And then we all shook hands with him and went off down the sidewalk till beyond Mr. Crofut's house, where the street curves. We ducked through Crofut's yard and up through the woods to the huge old oak tree on the knoll north of the playground.

8

THE ROC'S STILL THERE," said Joe, settling him-self on a branch above us. And sure enough, there it was, a huge quiet snow-covered mound.

"Still breathing, too," said Harry, wrapping his arm around a branch and focusing the binoculars.

"Look. Soldiers."

"Where?"

"Over by the corner of the school."

"They got a machine gun!" said Harry. "I can see it."

"The orchard!" yelled Dick. "Look. In the orchard."

A Sheridan tank was just heaving up over the ridge. It lumbered down between two rows of apple trees.

"There's cannons dug in all up and down the or-chard!" yelled Harry.

"Lemme try the glasses," said Joe, reaching down.

"I can't," said Harry. "They're my father's. He'd kill me if I broke them."

"He'll kill you for swiping them anyway. Lemme try them."

"They're loading one!" yelled Harry. "By the fence. Near the tank!"

And then he didn't say anything, his eyes glued to the binoculars. But we could hear him panting, so we figured something must be happening.

"Come on!" yelled Joe, nudging the back of Harry's neck with his toe. "What is it?"

"The General!" yelled Harry. "General Westinghouse! And a civilian's with him! Must be the Governor! They're by the cannon! General Westinghouse is handing the lanyard to the Governor! *Everybody hang on!*"

Albert tumbled past me. Dick landed on my back, sliding, clawing hold of my neck. . . . By the time we'd got untangled, flames were licking up around the jagged edges of a shell hole in the roof of the gym,

Albert was clambering back up over the lowest branch, and Joe was cheering, and Harry shouting,

"Again! They're loading! HANG ON!"

"O w w w w w!" yelled Albert.

A puff of smoke blossomed in the wall of the gym, bricks and dust fountained up.

"The tank!" yelled Joe.

Its turret was swiveling, its cannon dropping, dropping. I hugged the tree trunk. Dick hugged me.

"They're loading them all!" shouted Harry.

"They haven't hit him yet!" yelled Joe.

A shell burst on the roof of the gym.

"Grab me, Billy," cried Albert. "Geez, I'm missing *everything. Billy.*"

I reached down to grab his hand.

Albert sprawled on his back in the leaves. The tree shook, leaves fluttering down, brushing our faces. In the orchard, orange muzzle blasts bloomed like chrysanthemums. Explosions erupted all over the school, windows splintered, walls toppled, roofs caved in, doors blew out onto the playground.

"Direct hit!" yelled Joe.

"Right on top!"

Where the shell had hit the Roc, electric-blue feathers glared with startling brightness through the blanket of snow.

"Another!"

"They're zeroing in!"

I began to cry. I didn't want to see the Roc splattered and blown apart, like a chicken hit by a car. It hadn't eaten anybody. How did they *know* it was dangerous? Smoke and fire blanketed the shapeless mound. Dick was crying, too. Harry was yelling, Joe pounding a branch. And then, out of the midst of the smoke and exploding shells, the Roc's head appeared. A shell burst on its beak. It gawped. A dull roar grew behind us. The Roc blinked slowly.

"DUCK!" yelled Joe.

An earsplitting, shattering ROAARRRR! Three Phantom jets vanished over the roof of the school, banking up and away for another pass.

"Wow . . ."

ROAR! *Foosh, foosh, fooshfooshfoosh*. Rockets leaped from the second wave's wings. The Roc was buried in explosions, flying dirt, smoke, somersaulting rosebushes. ROAR! *Gloosh.* Napalm billowed across the playground, engulfing the Roc. ROAR! *Foosh, foosh, fooshfooshfoosh.* ROAR! *Gloosh.* ROAR! *Foosh, foosh, fooshfooshfoosh.* ROAR! *Foosh foosh.* ROAR! *Gloosh.*

Silence.

"Keep down. There may be more."

Silence. The crackle of flames, the rumble of collapsing walls. We peeked out from under our arms, a branch, from behind the tree trunk. Napalm burned quietly on the Roc, sending up thick clouds of oily smoke. Fires smoldered here and there in the rubble of the school. A muffled explosion. The boiler maybe.

"They didn't have to do it," Harry said, lowering the binoculars.

"That's just what they always do," said Dick. "They never give anybody a chance."

"I'm going home," I said.

"Wow," says Joe. "Did you see that? Fush, fush. Bammo!"

"What's happening?" Albert yelled up. "I can't see from down here. I'm coming up."

"They got him," said Harry, starting to climb down.

"Hey, lemme look through the glasses," said Joe. "I want to see what he looks like. Bammo!"

I started down.

Joe let out a strangled yell. The binoculars plummeted past me.

"He's . . . *Billy! Harry!* The . . . LOOK! LOOK!"

The Roc stood amidst the burning napalm, preening his electric-blue feathers. And then, suddenly, he began to run in a circle about the playground, leaping, leaping. And as he leaped, he screeched, a gigantic bird-screech:

"He s all right!" I yelled.

"They didn't kill him!" shouted Dick.

"He ain't even smudged!" yelled Joe.

We were all shouting and pounding each other on the back, jumping up and down on the branches. All except Albert, who lay unconscious under the tree, Harry's father's binoculars half-hidden under the leaves beside his head.

A siren wailed. We could see the soldiers retreating through the orchard, covered by the tank which gave

ground slowly, backing crookedly up the aisle between two rows of trees.

"They're withdrawing."

"What'll they do now?"

"Atom bomb."

"They couldn't. Not right in the middle of town."

"They could clear everybody out."

"We better get going."

"Yeah."

We slid and tumbled out of the tree. Albert was sitting up, gingerly touching a gash on his forehead.

"Geez, you could've killed me, Joe, dropping the binoculars like that."

"Yeah," said Joe. "Wow. Did you see them jets? Phoosh! Neeeeee-*ow!* Fush, fush, fushfushfush!"

Harry picked up the binoculars, brushing the leaves off them.

"You're bleeding," Dick said to Albert.

"Geez, I *know,*" said Albert. "And my legs are all wobbly."

We helped Albert find his glasses, which had fallen off, and then started down through the woods. The Roc had stopped running and leaping and was poking and scratching in the smoldering rubble, munching on the charred leg of a chair.

9

WHEN WE CAME BACK OUT onto the street through Crofut's yard, people were streaming along the sidewalks and in and out between lines of slowly moving cars and pickup trucks, National Guard tanks, weapons carriers and missile launchers, jeeps and ambulances. Everyone was carrying a suitcase or bundle or knapsack. Lots of people were pushing baby carriages or supermarket shopping carts or wheelbarrows piled high with their household stuff, a family portrait or television set roped on top. Even the little kids were dragging half-filled shopping bags or pushing loaded strollers.

"What's happening?" said Joe.

Albert took off his glasses and put them in his shirt pocket.

"It's what I said. They're evacuating the town."

We watched the people hurrying past.

"Why do they all look so fat?" asked Dick.

"They're all wearing extra clothes," said Harry.

Fur collars poked out from under raincoats; tweed suits had been pulled on over house dresses, evening gowns over slacks. Some people had four or five pairs of shoes dangling around their necks.

The cars and pickup trucks looked like sacks of sprouting potatoes, overloaded, sagging, bulging: mountains of furniture tied on the roofs, mattresses on the hoods; old people roped like deer to the fenders; a mirror glittering like an open door on a front grill. Sometimes a horse or cow ambled along behind, tethered to a back bumper, or hogs snuffled and rooted in a back seat. The people were all huddled and scrunched up inside among cardboard boxes, heaps of blankets and towels, squawking chickens, pots, pans, and dishes, heirloom lamps and chandeliers.

Every so often a car would break down, lurching to a

stop, steam leaking from the hood, the engine clattering and backfiring. Then a great honking and yelling would swell up while the driver, his wife and children hovering around him, frantically unroped the mattresses and flung up the hood. After a few minutes, if he couldn't get the car started again, the honking and yelling would let up. Other drivers would leave their cars and come to look in at his engine, muttering at each other, glancing back at the sky. And then all of a sudden you'd see men running and pushing and shoving, women and children would begin to scream, and the car would begin to rock, men swarming and pushing to get at it, and then over it would go on its side on somebody's lawn, and the blocked line of cars and trucks would inch forward again while the family — the mother and little girls and tottering grandfather all sobbing and hiccuping — pulled and yanked their stuff out of the overturned car, dividing it up into bundles so they could carry it on their backs.

People were trampling through flowerbeds and hedges, cutting cross-lots. Men and boys were running in and out of deserted houses, pearl necklaces dripping from their pockets, lugging color television sets, typewriters, radios, sewing machines.

Old Mrs. Crofut was rocking on her front porch. Every now and then she'd see somebody she knew in the crowd streaming past.

"You won't find no better place to live than South Sudbury, Henry Murray," she'd shout. "You mought better stay to home." Or, "Send me a postcard, Mrs. Ouhl. Don't forget an old body."

MPs on motorcycles threaded their way through the jam, gunning their engines. Drivers stood on top of their cars, trying to make out what was holding everything up. Every so often a wave of panic would sweep through the crowd.

"It's coming!"

People would try to run, hobbled by their suitcases and bundles, their extra overcoats and skirts. A shopping cart would buck over, spilling into the street; a man trundling a loaded wheelbarrow, glancing back up at the sky for the Roc, would run down a child. Screams. People diving, scrambling on hands and knees under the nearest porches, crouching in the street over their children to protect them, running, running, falling, stumbling, an old man trying to haul his wife back onto her feet amid the rushing crowd, little kids jouncing fearfully along on their fathers' shoulders, car doors slamming, swinging wide as the occupants fled to huddle under porches and peer white-eyed out at the sky; the soldiers on the trucks slamming home their rifle bolts, turning about, jostling each other as they searched the sky for the Roc.

And then a helicopter would clatter by overhead or a motorcycle ridden by a goggled, helmeted MP would come threading through the crowd, in and out between trucks and cars and baby carriages, up the hill and on toward the school. The panic would peter out, people emerging from under porches, picking up bundles, suit-

ig back into their cars. Someone would
man pick his wife up; the jam of cars and
uld inch forward, the soldiers slouching
he sides of the trucks, gazing listlessly down at
the arms of trudging people, whistling at pretty girls.

Joe was scared.

"I'm going," he says. "Geez, look at them running, everyone screaming." His face was as pale as an onion. "We'll get trampled. Let's go back into the woods."

He turned and started back around the house.

"He's scared of the crowd," said Dick. "Remember the basketball game last winter? We'll come get you when we're ready to leave," he called to Joe.

Joe disappeared around the corner of the house. The rest of us sat down on the porch steps and watched the crowd streaming by, old Mrs. Crofut's rocker creaking behind us. Every so often a kid from our class would go by with his parents. Judy Schwartz and her older sister and two brothers waved to us from the top of their father's station wagon, where they were riding among trunks and boxes and chairs. Six or seven sheep bleated inside the station wagon, poking their black noses out the slitted windows. Jenny Lorimer and her father and mother had rolled up the windows in their car. Her parents stared straight ahead, but Jenny gazed bleakly out at us, red-eyed, tear-stained, and tangle-haired. Then Arnie Bentley's father's pickup came along with the raccoon tails and the American flag on the aerial, and the spotlights and streamers and Day-Glo decals. We ran and looked in the back and sure enough, there was Arnie, all huddled up under his cowboy hat in a corner. So Albert asked Mr. Bentley if he'd give us a ride and he says, sure, hop in, and Mrs. Bentley asked us where our parents were.

"Home, I guess," Harry says.

"Well, you sit right down there, all of you. They must be worried sick."

While the truck inched along, we tried to persuade Arnie to come out from under the cowboy hat and pleaded with the soldiers in the troop carrier beside us to fire off their guns, till Albert said,

"Joe. We forgot Joe."

"We gotta go back."

We all tumbled out of the truck, Mrs. Bentley yelling after us, and dodged through the crowd and across a couple of yards to the Crofuts'. Joe was sitting on the back doorsill, pale and shivering.

"Geez," he said when he saw us, "I thought you'd run out on me when I couldn't hear you shouting anymore."

y's giving us a ride in his truck. Come

bing into that crowd," Joe says, hugging his
shivering. "Everybody all excited like that,
sc… …g and shoving."

So we all watched him for a moment.

"Let's go around by the railroad station," Albert says. "Across the tracks. There won't be any crowd that way."

We set off. There were a few people hurrying along the alley by Mack Molding, and we could hear the murmur of the crowd on the street all the time, but Joe began to get his color back and wasn't shivering so bad. We started down the hill behind the old summer hotel through the weeds and sumac. Joe stopped when he saw where we were headed. Now and then you could catch a glimpse of the crowd down on Main Street through the leaves.

"I'm staying here," he says.

"Geez. Come on, will ya?"

"We got to cross the street to get home."

He was hugging himself and trembling again.

"I'll stay here. No one's home probably anyway. It's my mother's Daughters of Italy morning."

"She won't be at a meeting with all this going on.

They're evacuating the town. We'll get left behind.

But he just knelt there beside a bush, hugging himself.

"What'll we do?" said Dick. "We can't just leave him."

"Come on. We'll pull him along," said Albert.

But he fought us off, punching and kicking. He was crying now. We were all beginning to get scared. I didn't think my mother would go off without me, but suppose someone had told her I was dead or something? I didn't want to get home and find the back door swinging open and the house echoing and empty, a bird fluttering against the mirror in the front hall, trying to get out.

Albert motioned us aside. Joe was huddled up by the bush, his head between his knees.

"We'll have to tie him," whispered Albert. "Harry, there's rope on the delivery platform back at Mack Molding. I saw it when we came past. You and Dick run back and get it. Billy, we got to rip our shirttails for a gag and blindfold. Here." He clawed up his sweater and pulled out his shirttail. "You got a knife?"

When Harry and Dick came back with the rope, we all got around behind Joe and snuck up on him and *pounced!*

s!" yelled Albert.

or his ankle and got kicked in the cheek.

rying to wrestle a dog into a bathtub.

t go now!" yelled Harry.

we got him down under us. We were panting and perspiring.

"The rope," gasped Albert.

We tied his hands and feet. He'd gone limp.

"Now," says Albert. "Do you want the gag and blindfold?"

Joe blinked up at us and then nodded.

"Okay," says Albert, standing up. "He's all set. Lock hands. Harry and Billy under his shoulders, Dick and me at his feet."

So we lugged him down the hill, slithering and sliding, and up the alley between Howard's Store and the hotel out to Main Street. We put him down on the sidewalk, resting and waiting for the crowd to jam up and stop. Then we rushed him across, threading our way among the baby carriages and cars and missile launchers and trucks, and staggered through the filigree iron gate into the cemetery.

"Whew," said Dick.

We laid him on the tomb of

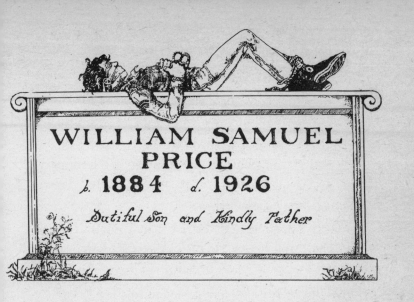

WILLIAM SAMUEL
PRICE
b. 1884   d. 1926
Dutiful Son and Kindly Father

and flopped down in the grass. Beyond the wall people began to scream, horns honked, a man vaulted over the wall and ran through the cemetery. Mr. Watkins kicked through the gate, his wife and their son, Sammy, who was in tenth grade, behind him. Sammy was pulling a lawn cart piled with furniture and stuff. Near us the cart hit a stone and overturned.

"Pop!" yelled Sammy. His father and mother looked back and then stopped and ran to him, righting the cart, flinging pillows and blankets back into it.

A helicopter clattered by overhead. A voice boomed from a loudspeaker.

"Do not panic. Do not panic. Proceed in an orderly

fashion. The monster is still at the school. He has not left the north playground. Do not panic. Remain calm."

The helicopter moved off up the highway. Mr. and Mrs. Watkins stopped flinging stuff into the cart and started discussing what they should do.

"Hey, Sammy," says Albert, who knew him because Sammy sometimes helped out at his uncle's store. "What's everybody panicking for?"

"The bird mangled Mr. Stanwick's leg."

"Who said? The troopers tried it with meat yesterday and it wouldn't touch it."

"Mr. Stanwick went back to his office to rescue some papers or something. It was the only part of the building that wasn't wrecked by the guns. But while he was cleaning out his drawers, the Roc stuck its head in the window. So Mr. Stanwick crawled under the desk and the Roc chomped down on it and got Mr. Stanwick's leg instead. Mr. Rushmore saw the whole thing. He was helping Mr. Stanwick."

"I wish it'd been his head," said Dick.

"So what's everybody panicking about?"

"I don't know. They're afraid the Roc might start in on them next, I guess. They're throwing away chairs and mirrors. You should see them."

His father called him and they tied the furniture and

stuff back on the lawn cart and went off through the cemetery. We took Joe's gag and blindfold off and asked him if he wanted to walk now.

"Put it back on," he croaked. "Put it back on. I'm not so scared that way. I imagine I'm sleeping in a boat far out at sea."

So we lugged him across the cemetery and boosted him over the wall and through somebody's backyard and across Salem Street to his house, where his father and brothers were loading up their panel truck in the driveway and his mother was weeping and wailing on the front porch among his sisters.

"Here he is, Mrs. Fornaro," called Albert.

She looked up and screamed and then rushed down the porch steps, fat and disheveled.

"He's dead! Oh, he's dead!"

"He was scared of the crowds," said Albert, kneeling to untie the gag and blindfold.

She stood over them, clutching her hanky to her bosom, sort of in a state of expectant shock, I guess. Then when Albert pulled the blindfold off and she saw Joe open his eyes and blink, she fell on her knees beside him, hugging him up.

So we shook hands with Joe's father and his brothers, and the oldest brother gave us each a quarter and one of his married sisters rummaged in a box in the back of the truck and handed us a loaf of bread and half a salami. Then we went off down the street.

But we hadn't gone far before Joe's mother came shouting after us and asked us where we were going and where were our parents, and after we'd told her and she'd made sure we knew the way home and that we would go cross-lots, not through the crowds on the roads, she hugged each of us and thanked us for bringing Joe home and then hesitated, started to call one of her sons, and then looked at us, standing there in the street, Dick and Harry and Albert and me, and said:

"Do you know the way? You're sure? Sure, you'll make it home. Don't go near the river now."

So we set off.

When we got to the Sandgate crossroads, we all hunkered down under the lightning-blasted tree and passed the loaf of bread and the salami around, wrenching off bites with our teeth and watching the traffic on the road. It was still bumper to bumper headed west in both lanes. But now the National Guard trucks were loaded with civilians — men, women, and children — and their belongings, and people were crowded on the roofs of cars and hanging on all over the weapons carriers and tanks and missile launchers. A long column of soldiers marched beside the road. Every so often there'd be a jam-up, and people would drop off the sides of tanks and missile launchers to stretch; fathers would lead little boys off into the bushes. Nobody was panicking, but I noticed they all kept a sharp eye on the sky, especially back toward town.

"Dick," said Harry after a while, "what do you say if I come home with you?"

"What about your parents?" I said.

He shrugged.

We all stood up, brushing crumbs off our shirts, hitching up our pants.

"Who'll take what's left?" asked Albert.

"We'll flip for it."

Albert and I lost, so Harry stuffed the bread into his shirt and handed the salami to Dick and they went off up the Sandgate Road.

I couldn't figure Harry. I mean, I knew he was a loner. I'd heard his parents didn't care what time he came home at night. Joe'd told me once he was always hanging around people's houses at suppertime, waiting to be invited in to eat with them. So I guess there was something wrong in his family. But here he was *deserting* his parents. The town was being evacuated, everybody was leaving, saving what little they could, and Harry acted like he didn't even *care* where his parents were. I mean, my mother is nervous and all, and my father always backs her up even if she's wrong. Like she'll be upset because he's going away so she'll yell at me when I start downstairs at bedtime to get my rocket model, even though she's told me five minutes before I could; so I'll yell back, not stopping, and my father'll thunder at me, and I'll trudge muttering back past him into my room. But still I wouldn't desert them in a crisis. Just like they wouldn't desert me. I don't know. *I* couldn't figure it.

Anyway, Harry and Dick went off up the Sandgate Road and Albert and me kept on to my house.

⟨10⟩

ALBERT'S MOTHER was standing in the kitchen door, looking up the road.

"You get in to your mother, young man," she says to me. "Running off like that, scaring us half to death. She's been in tears ever since we woke up."

I slid by her into the kitchen.

Slap! behind me. "Albert O'Reilly, I'll tan your *hide* for this." *Slap!* "What do you mean running off like that?" *Slap!* "Leaving a note like that behind." *Slap!* "Saying you're going to school *early!*" *Slap!*

Oh *boy,* my mother's hair was draggling all over her face, and her eyes were red and puffy. She was sitting at the kitchen table.

"Billy. Billy."

She reached out to hug me, but I stopped by the sink. I was sorry I'd scared her, and I was glad she and Albert's mother hadn't left without us, but I don't know, I didn't want her to hug me and cry all over me.

"Oh. Oh."

She began to sob again, covering her face with both hands.

"I'm all right, Mom."

"Oh Billy. I thought you'd been hoo hoo hoo hoo hoo . . ."

She went off again. Abigail stared at her from her playpen. I heard Albert in the entryway trying to explain what had happened to his mother.

"Oh Billy, I was so worried."

She got out her crumpled handkerchief and dabbed at her cheeks.

"Billy, why didn't you *tell* me? I could have explained."

"Mommy cry?" said Abigail.

"Hoo hoo." She wiped her eyes. "All better. Mommy not crying now. Hoo hoo hoo hoo hoo."

So I patted her shoulder and said I was sorry and, you know, I'd never go off like that again and I was sorry, I forgot, you know, that she'd worry, patting her shoulder.

"Oh, I was so worried, Billy. I didn't know what would happen, and I couldn't leave Abby."

"Yeah. Yeah, I know."

"And it was still dark outside. We didn't know where you'd gone."

She hugged me. And then she unhugged me so she could look at me, pushing my hair out of my face and wondering if I was really all right, and hugged me again, and made me pull up my shirt to see if I had any wounds, and had I gotten in any poison ivy, and then she remembered how when she'd woken up to find me gone in the early dawn, she'd realized that my father wasn't there either. So she broke down again, hugging me, sobbing hoo hoo hoo hoo hoo over my shoulder.

"Geez," I said, "cut it out, Mom, will you? I'm all right."

I mean I was sorry for her, but she was smothering me. Wasn't I all right? So she'd been worried. I was *back! Safe!*

I wrenched away.

"Cut it out! Do you have to cry *all over me*?"

"Don't you speak to your mother that way, young man!" says Mrs. O'Reilly, coming into the kitchen. "She's been worried *sick* over you!"

Slap!

Me this time.

"Hey!"

My mother looked up.

"Now you say you're sorry properly, young man," says Mrs. O'Reilly.

"Did you slap Billy?" said my mother. "Did you?"

"Yes," says Mrs. O'Reilly. Albert was peering around her. "And don't you worry, Mrs. —"

"What right have you to slap my son?"

She wasn't crying now.

"I don't know what you mean."

"Do you *think*, do you think for a moment I will permit my son to be slapped by any . . . any *woman* who can't control herself?"

"I'm sure I don't . . ."

"Do you think I will permit him to be *harried*, and *badgered*, by any . . . any *woman* who . . ."

"*Woman?*" says Mrs. O'Reilly. "Just what do you mean by that?"

Her face was as red as hamburger.

My mother was standing now, her fists clenched at her sides.

"I mean *just* that," she says. "*Woman.*"

She sort of spat it out, like a peach pit.

"What *right* have you to call me that?"

"*Woman.*"

Their noses were almost touching. Mrs. O'Reilly spoke through clenched teeth:

"If you think for an instant that I . . ."

"*Woman.*"

"She shouldn't call my mother that," said Albert to me. We were watching by the refrigerator.

"She shouldn't have slapped me."

"You deserved it just as much as me."

"Yeah, but *your* mother shouldn't have slapped me. People aren't supposed to slap other people's children."

"They are when no one else will. Your mother's a weak fish. Everybody says so."

"Fink!" I yelled.

And just at that instant, Albert and me about to fling

ourselves on each other, our mothers red-faced, nose to nose, the door banged open and Mr. O'Reilly called, "Anybody home?" and stomped into the kitchen in his hunting clothes and boots.

"Hello," he says. "Everybody's here, eh. How are you, Mrs. Travis? Billy. Whatta you say, boy?" rumpling Albert's hair, "I'm back early, dear." He kissed his wife's

cheek. Nobody said anything. "Well. I heard what happened. Saw Clem Barney on the road. We'd better pack on up. Though there doesn't seem to be any immediate danger. Clem said Bill Edgerton told him the troopers had experimented with the bird and didn't believe it was carnivorous. Is Mr. Travis back from California, Mrs. Travis?"

Nobody said anything. I couldn't look at Albert. Geez, he was my best friend, and we'd almost got into a fight over *nothing;* our *mothers.*

"Well!" says Mr. O'Reilly, puzzled, looking from one to the other of us.

"Oh, Mrs. O'Reilly," said my mother suddenly, "it's . . ."

"I can't think . . ." said Mrs. O'Reilly, "the excitement, the . . ."

"I'm so *sorry,*" says my mother.

"It was thoughtless of me. Mr. Travis away . . ."

"I certainly didn't mean to call you a *woman.* I was just carried . . ."

"I know you didn't. I know . . ."

So they went on like that for a while, and then Mrs. O'Reilly said, My, we'd better get those dishes washed, and my mother said, No, she wouldn't *permit* her to help, and so they protested and excused themselves and apologized some more, turning on the water, scraping plates into the garbage, till Mr. O'Reilly said:

"Hey, hey, hey, hey. We've got to get going. Mrs. Travis, you and the children had better come with us. Albert, you stay here till your mother and I come back. You and Billy help his mother with her packing."

❦ 11 ❧

THREE WEEKS LATER Albert and me clung to a scraggly oak growing out of the top of a mammoth boulder on the peak of Bald Mountain. Thousands and thousands of people draped the tops of mountains all around us as far as we could see, trampling down the blueberry bushes at Kelly Stand; like white ants on the face of Flag Rock in the distance, the sunlight glinting on binoculars, cameras, telescopes, thermoses.

Hawkers trudged through the crowds.

"Hot dogs. Hot dogs."

"Hey, get your cold beer."

"Peanuts."

"Hey, ice cream, ice cream."

"Sunshades."

"Soda."

"Popcorn, peanuts."

"Souvenirs."

Eight miles away, among the tiny toy white houses

and late autumn maples of South Sudbury, the electric-blue Roc glittered in the sunlight like a spot of oil. Two helicopters hovered like dragonflies over him.

Through the Air Force telescopes you could see him feeding on a chiffonier in the rubble of Mr. Atkins's house, and behind him, winding all the way up the hill to the school, a litter of roofless, gutted houses. Remnants of furniture were scattered about on the scraggly, overgrown lawns — a half-chewed mahogany table, an overturned Barcalounger, the glinting glass door of a china cabinet. Weeds were sprouting in the cracks of the asphalt driveways.

"It's not really fair," said Albert suddenly. "They should at least let him get as far as Fleischmann's Furniture Store."

"Yeah. Sort of like a last meal."

"My father read Dick and me an article from a magazine telling about the different kinds of furniture he likes. It said he saves the antiques — you know, the old stuff — for dessert. But my father said it's a lot of hooey. Didn't he, Dick?"

"Yeah," said Dick.

Dick was sitting in the weeds at the bottom of the boulder, scratching in the dirt with a stick. He was real low. The night of the evacuation his father and brothers

and Ned Myers had snuck back into town to loot,
taking him and Harry with them. But the National
Guard had surprised them leaving Howard's Store in
the moonlight with two wheelbarrows piled high with
the cash register and stuff, and Dick's brother Kenny
had been shot in the leg and all of them captured,
though Ned Myers not till next morning because he'd
hid in the drain under the highway. Dick's brothers
and father were sent to jail, and then the police thought
once they'd got started they might as well finish the
job and sent his mother to the state hospital as an alco-
holic, and Dick went to live with Albert.

"Is it almost time?" asked Albert.

"Five minutes."

"Hey, look, there's Joe."

Joe was sulking beside his mother. Ever since we'd brought him home that day, she hadn't let him out of her sight.

"He don't look so good," said Albert.

"Yeah, he's a lot thinner. Hey, Joe!"

We all yelled and waved at him. He looked around and then waved listlessly.

The army loudspeakers crackled:

"Ladies and gentlemen, the tactical atomic device will be detonated at precisely 9:23 Eastern Standard Time. Mission Control reports that all systems are go. The F–111B which will transport the device to target left Andrews Air Force Base on schedule. Commander Wally Fosden in Air Force Helicopter Two reports that the target is munching quietly on a horsehair sofa which it extracted at dawn from the attic of 154 School Street, the former residence of Mr. and Mrs. William Atkins."

The loudspeakers crackled.

"The time is now D minus four minutes and counting. The President has just taken his seat in the grandstand on Red Mountain. He is accompanied by the Joint Chiefs of Staff and the leaders of the Senate and House of Representatives. The Secretary-General of the

United Nations and the various ambassadors and other dignitaries present in the grandstand gave the President a standing ovation."

"My father says he's a fink," I said.

"Because he ordered the army to kill the Roc?"

"Yeah, but my father says he was a fink before that, too."

"They shouldn't kill it," muttered Dick suddenly from below.

Dick was real upset about the Roc, too. I mean, none of us thought the government should kill it, but Dick got in fights about it. He'd sit in a corner, listening to some kid arguing with Albert or me, rubbing his nose and mumbling about how "they should give it a chance, they weren't giving it a chance, maybe it wasn't so bad after all." And then the kid would say something like, well, people shot partridges, didn't they, the Roc was no . . . and all of a sudden Dick would be on top of him, punching and kicking and biting and pulling hair. He hadn't wanted to come up on the mountain with us. But I guess he hadn't wanted to stay home either, waiting in an empty house in an empty town for the dull thud of the explosion miles away. On the trail coming up he'd lagged behind all the way, biting his nails and kicking rocks into the bushes.

Albert let go of the tree a moment to push his glasses back up on his nose. He was hugging the tree with all his arms and legs; he said he didn't want to fall and miss everything again.

"My father says the scientists don't really know anything about the Roc. As long as it's peaceful, just eating furniture and hopping and dancing about, they should just study it. Maybe when it breathes, it purifies the air or something. But everybody's too scared."

The loudspeakers crackled.

"D minus two and still counting. Captain C. C. "Shorty" Masters aboard the F-111B command bomber reports that the atomic device is ticking nicely. Scientists at North-American-Douglas in San Diego, the prime contractor, indicate that all systems are go at this time. The observation helicopters are now being withdrawn."

We watched the two helicopters come slowly toward us up the valley. They passed overhead, clattering.

"D minus one and still counting. Will all observers please put on the green radiation glasses provided courtesy of North-American-Douglas and the United States Air Force. The forward observation bunker on Sudbury Mountain reports that the target is now stooping slightly to peer into the second-floor windows of 152 School Street, the former residence of Mrs. Agnes Rapp, widow of Samuel Rapp, late president of the New York, New Haven, and Calcutta Railroad. D minus twenty seconds, nineteen, eighteen, seventeen, sixteen . . ."

We could hear a growing roar behind us.

". . . fifteen, fourteen, thirteen, twelve, eleven, ten, nine . . ."

The announcer was shouting now, trying to make himself heard over the roar of the F-111B.

". . . eight, seven, six . . ."

We ducked. The leaves fluttered in the blast of sound as the F-111B shot overhead, diminishing suddenly toward the spot of electric blue in the distance . . .

a burst of light obliterated the daylight, whitening trees, valleys, mountains, the silent staring throngs on the mountains . . .

The autumn hills and fields, the roads, crowds, blue sky returned. A cloud of smoke mushroomed up from the trees which hid South Sudbury. A church steeple on the outskirts of town dissolved in splinters. The cloud boiled and boiled, spreading, streaks of smoke shooting out of it. And suddenly we were engulfed in sound. Albert tumbled past me. I clung to the scraggly tree. Wind streamed through my clothes like icy water; hats, sandwiches, paper cups, jackets, hot dogs, scarfs flew past. Waves of sound whelmed over me. Echoes caromed through the valleys. And then suddenly there was quiet, the echoes dying away, sandwich wrappers fluttering down. Over South Sudbury the mushroom cloud began to disperse as the high-altitude winds struck it.

"Wow," I whispered.

Dick screamed.

"LOOK!"

In the midst of the boiling cloud a spot of electric blue, growing, growing, emerging from the cloud, now over the smoldering rubble of South Sudbury, soaring clumsily, climbing . . .

"The Roc!" screamed Dick. "The Roc!"

The Roc came steadily on toward the throngs on the mountains, gigantic, electric blue, leaving behind the raw circle of destruction — uprooted trees, twisted bridges, blackened fields, burning barns — gaining altitude, its tiny dodo's wings beating madly, its great yellow basketball eyes blinking slowly, indifferently.

A hesitant movement in the crowds, a shrinking back, almost involuntary, fear of the Roc gradually overpowering the shock of the explosion and blasts of light and sound . . .

The mountains echoed, ponds rippled.

"RUN!"

The crowd stampeded over the brow of the mountain, leaving the trampled underbrush littered with picnic baskets, binoculars, lawn chairs.

The gigantic, electric-blue bird approached, growing huger and huger every moment as it bundled through the sky toward us.

"It's as big as Yankee Stadium!" yelled Dick.

The last remnants of the crowd, old ladies, injured children, hobbled over the brow of the mountain. Distant screams echoed up the steep sides. A siren wailed on the highway far below. We could hear the great bellows of the Roc's breathing now. And suddenly it was upon us.

Huge, huge. Filling the sky overhead. Darkening the mountaintop. And all we saw was blue, blue, blue. The great feathered breast and underpinnings of the Roc. An Alpine meadow.

And he was gone. We stared into the clear November sky again, far up in the stratosphere a fleeing vapor trail.

We turned to look after him. Already he was no bigger than an elephant. He shrank and shrank. I lost him for a moment against the sky, picked him out again, a tiny speck, and he was gone. Screams echoed from the other side of the mountain. I climbed down off the rock and helped Albert up, and we went off to find our parents. Like sleepwalkers. Dazed, wobbling.

⟨12⟩

WELL, everything's back to normal again. Or almost. We're back in school. Split sessions in the Grange Hall in Cambridge. But they think we'll be able to move back to South Sudbury in a couple of months. The government's going to rebuild everything just like it was except where the town decides on something better. Like the new school probably won't be anything like the old one. They're already having endless meetings about it. The old school and playground are going to be made into a national park.

Miss Kinnell's still our teacher. But she's lost weight. Mr. Firuski's back. Mr. Stanwick's become a sort of national hero because so far he's the only person ever bitten by the Roc. The Senate voted him a gold-plated crutch and a pension, and he went on television and told about his experiences, lying a lot, and thanked everyone for their kind letters and gifts, and the government for the pension, but he said he wasn't going to leave his work, he loved children too much. So we all groaned, Albert and Dick and me and Joe, and turned off the television and went off by the river to hunt frogs.

The Roc's been seen only once since the bombing. Some mountain climbers in the Alps saw him through a snow squall floating high over Mont Blanc. Nobody knows what he'll do — whether he'll land somewhere else on earth, or fly off into space, or shrink back into nothingness, vanishing as he came. Some people have decided he's the son of God, sent down to redeem the world again; they stamp about on the tops of parked cars in long white robes, their noses painted electric blue, waving their arms and preaching. There are occasional panics: riots in Istanbul, San Diego, Brussels, Karachi. Lots of people have built bird-shelters in their backyards; the government handed out a tin helmet to anybody who wanted one. Some people even burned their furniture and eat and sleep on the floor now. My father says it's all nonsense, but I notice he sets big over-stuffed chairs out on the front and back porches every night before he comes up to bed. As decoys, I guess, to distract the Roc so we'll have time to escape out a window if it alights some night on the front lawn. The scientists have got a whole lot of new stuff to try on him if he ever lands anywhere again. But I bet it won't work.

I think the Roc is like the Russians or children, just something people have to learn to live with.

Dick's still staying at Albert's house. Every weekend he goes all the way to Shushan to visit his sister Junie, who's living with a foster family there. Joe's mother is letting him out once in a while now. Albert and me are about the same. Harry Walters's parents sent him away to live with his aunt and uncle way out somewhere in western New York State, so we never see him anymore.

I suppose the Roc'll never come back to South Sudbury. Albert and Dick and Joe and me all hope he will. Reading, writing, arithmetic. If it wasn't for Saturdays and Sundays and vacations, I'd run off, go looking for the Roc maybe. Albert and Dick and Joe say the same thing.